An Altered Existence:
Fictitious Stories About Faces from the Past

Stories & Altered Photo Illustrations by

Melody M. Nuñez

For José Nuñez

CONTENTS

AUTHOR'S NOTE

This collection of short stories is a work of fiction. The stories were inspired by the photos that accompany them, and are strictly products of my imagination. I purchased the photos in antique stores and at flea markets, and can say with certainty that the actual people photographed weren't the people I created in these stories. I'd like to apologize to the individuals who became unsavory characters, and thank all those featured in the photos for inspiring me with their silent mystery.

I've tried to be historically accurate wherever possible. I hope you'll indulge me any inaccuracies in the interest of some creative fun.

MMN

Distant Relatives

Lori let out an excited squeak when she read the results of her pregnancy test and saw the + in the results window. She and her husband, Chris, had been trying for a second child ever since their five-year-old Hannah had turned two. Lori had been getting a bit nervous. Really nervous, truth be told. They had their hearts set on having two children, preferably a boy and a girl. Their window of opportunity was closing bit by bit as Lori approached her fortieth birthday and her fertility dropped off by the day. They had decided the stress and frenetic pace of their lives in Manhattan might be hampering the conception of their second child and set about moving to a more leisurely paced life in the country. They'd always hoped to raise their family in the country anyway, and Chris' recent inheritance made their dream possible.

Six months ago, Lori, Chris, and Hannah Miner had packed up and moved to a rambling farmhouse in upstate New York. Known locally as Miner Farm, the house and surrounding acreage had been in Chris' family for more than a hundred years. Twelve months earlier, Chris' grandmother, Muriel, had died and left the home to Chris. Although Chris and Lori missed the sweet matriarch of the Miner family, they were tickled pink to have been given the farm. They'd spent a small fortune updating the home before they actually moved in with Hannah; their improvements had included an upgraded electrical system, new plumbing, central heating and air, and a modernized kitchen. They tried to maintain the rustic charm of the home while making it more livable and ensuring that it was up to current safety codes. They'd kept the original hardwood floors, marveling that the craftsmanship and materials had held up so well for more than a century.

As Lori looked at the pregnancy test results, she wondered if she could wait for Chris to get home that night to share the wonderful news of their new baby with him. He would be ecstatic too. She was tempted to call him right away, but decided she'd rather tell him in person so they could celebrate – with sparkling cider instead of champagne in deference to the little one she was carrying. By her estimation, she was about six weeks pregnant. As Lori put away the pregnancy test and threw away the related packaging, she heard Hannah's voice down the hall and smiled to think of her little girl playing quietly in her room after waking from her afternoon nap. Lori stepped out of the bathroom and walked quietly down the hall so she could peek in on Hannah before her daughter actually saw her. Hannah was sitting at the little table in the corner of her room, having a tea party with the mini tea set her maternal grandmother had given her for her fourth birthday.

"Would you like sugar in your tea, Emily?" Hannah said to the chair on her left. Apparently Emily did want sugar, as Hannah proceeded to mime adding two spoonfuls of sugar to the cup designated as Emily's. Hannah then turned to the right and asked a question of a second guest.

"Would you like another cookie, Joseph? Oh, you'd like two? Of course you can have two more cookies – dinner won't be ready for hours." Lori smiled to herself as Hannah doled out two invisible cookies to her guest, Joseph. Not only did Hannah have impeccable manners, she also knew better than to ruin everyone's appetite for dinner. Lori and Chris would certainly share a chuckle over this tonight after they'd put Hannah to bed. They had no concerns about whether or not she'd be a good sister or whether she'd welcome a new baby. They suspected she'd handle the new arrival with the maturity and grace that had seemed to surround Hannah from birth. She had her fussy moments, to be sure, but they were few and far between.

"Hey, sweetie, did you have a good nap?" Lori asked Hannah.

Turning to the doorway, Hannah smiled and said "Yes, mommy, and now I'm having a tea party with my friends, Emily and Joseph."

Lori remembered Hannah mentioning these two friends before and guessed that Hannah had created two imaginary friends to fill in for actual playmates. "That's wonderful, Hannah, and you're playing so nicely with your imaginary friends. I'm proud of you for being such a good hostess!"

Hannah looked a bit puzzled as she glanced to her left and right, then back to her mother in the doorway. Her little brow furrowed as she said, "Mommy, Emily and Joseph aren't imaginary. They're real. Emily is almost four, and Joseph is eight. They're brother and sister and live here in the house with us. Don't you see them?"

Lori looked at each of the vacant chairs to show Hannah that she was listening to her and wanted to see them, but had to admit that she didn't see either sibling.

"I'm sorry, Hannah. Maybe they're magic and can only be seen by little girls named Hannah."

Hannah looked at her in exasperation, as if that was the stupidest thing she'd ever heard, and wordlessly went back to her tea party. Lori chalked Emily and Joseph up to her child's active imagination and headed downstairs to get dinner ready. Chris would be home in an hour and a half, coming in on the 6:30 train, and she wanted to have a nice meal ready for him after his long workday and commute. Thankfully, he was able to work from home sometimes, but today had not been one of those days.

When Chris walked through the door and sniffed the savory scent of Lori's homemade lasagna, he greeted her with an even bigger smile than usual. Lori grabbed the combination briefcase and laptop bag from her husband's hands and planted a juicy kiss on his lips before stowing the bag away.

"Lori, you must've been reading my mind. I was dreaming about your homemade lasagna earlier today. What a treat! I'm so hungry I could probably eat the whole pan all by myself!" Chris gazed appreciatively at his wife, and his stomach seconded what he'd just said by letting out a loud rumble. They looked at each other and cracked up at the timing, then Lori gave him a playful swat on the rump.

"The lasagna is nearly done, and everything will be on the table in about fifteen minutes. Go play with Hannah for a few minutes, okay? She's been counting down the hours until you got home. She's been keeping herself entertained by playing with Emily and Joseph, but you know how much she adores her daddy!"

Chris gave her a faux-modest look, as if to say, "Can you blame her?" and then asked who Emily and Joseph were.

"Oh, they're her imaginary friends. They were all having a tea party today after Hannah's nap," Lori explained. "She seemed offended when I called them her imaginary friends. She insisted that they're real – a brother and sister who live here in the house with us. What an imagination! Do you think she'll grow up to be a writer like her mommy?" Lori had been scribbling in various notebooks from the time she'd learned to read and write and earned extra money for the household by writing occasional magazine articles on a freelance basis.

"Perhaps," Chris said. "Or maybe she'll be an accounting genius like her daddy!"

"Well, Mr. Accounting Genius, why don't you scoot on upstairs and see what Hannah's up to? I'll call you two when everything's ready." Lori winked at Chris as he made his way out of the room.

Minutes later, she heard Hannah screech "Daddy!" and smiled as she heard the child's peals of laughter. Chris was undoubtedly tickling her silly.

Later that evening, husband and wife relaxed on the sofa in the living room, limbs comfortably intertwined. They'd had an incredible dinner, gave Hannah a bath, and after the three of them had read Hannah's favorite book *The Giving Tree*, they'd tucked their precious daughter in bed. She'd been asleep in a matter of minutes, faintly illuminated by the teddy bear lamp they'd switched to the nightlight setting.

"This has been a perfect evening – a great ending to a super hectic day," Chris said, his voice thick with relaxation as his head lolled back on the couch cushion behind him.

Lori hated to disturb his relaxed state, but knew he wouldn't mind this particular interruption. "Honey, I hate to nag you, but do you think you'll have time to paint the spare bedroom this weekend? I'm not sure if we should paint it pink or blue, but I think it's going to be occupied soon."

Chris' head snapped up and he looked at her in surprise. "Lori, what are you saying? Are you pregnant?" Seeing his wife nod and seeing the excited grin on her face, he whooped for joy and then planted an enthusiastic kiss on her lips. They chattered to each other excitedly, and Lori brought out two champagne flutes and a bottle of sparkling cider to celebrate. They toasted each other and their unborn child, reflecting on their many blessings.

"All our hard 'work' has finally paid off," Chris said, leering at his amused wife.

"Yes, Chris, you were right – practice makes perfect!" Lori couldn't help but laugh at her goofy husband. "Now, if you're through reliving how we conceived this child, might we focus on the baby itself for a moment? I think we might want to delay the big announcement for a while."

They discussed the matter for a few minutes and decided to hold off telling everyone, including Hannah, until Lori entered her fourth month of pregnancy. She'd been pregnant once before Hannah was conceived, and they had mistakenly told everyone about the pregnancy while they were still in the first trimester, which had made it that much harder when they lost the baby in an early miscarriage. They didn't want to go through all that again, so they decided to wait another two and a half months to share the news, if they could.

The conversation drifted to baby names, and Lori mentioned an idea that had come to her earlier that day. "Why don't I look for some Miner family names in that box of photos, books, and historical documents – the one that's tucked in the closet of the guest room? It might be nice to have an old-fashioned name from your side of the family since we've been lucky enough to come to live here at Miner Farm."

Chris squeezed Lori's hand and said, "That's a wonderful idea, Lori. I think Grandma Muriel would love it too."

Lori made good on her suggestion the very next day. After Hannah laid down for a nap, Lori made her way into the guest room two doors down from Hannah's room. Lori kept the door wide open so she could listen for her daughter, then grabbed the box from the closet. She pulled everything out and stacked it in one corner of the queen-size bed. She then went about sorting the items by type.

First there was a thick stack of assorted documents, including decorative and ornate marriage certificates and baptism certificates. There were a few books, including a well-loved Bible, and three photo albums filled with black-and-white snapshots. Lori smiled with pleasure at the sight of a small, framed photo of Miner Farm, likely taken shortly after the house was built in 1885. She and Chris would have to find a place of honor to hang the precious keepsake. Finally, there was a stack of formal portraits that Lori recognized as cabinet cards.

Approximately four inches by six inches, the cabinet cards consisted of a black and white photo mounted onto thick cardstock for stability. The photo on top of the stack featured a young boy standing with a baby girl, who was sitting propped up on a chair. Lori admired the adorable children in their antiquated clothes before putting the photos aside. She promised herself she'd look through all the cabinet cards after she'd reviewed some of the documents. Perhaps there were names jotted on the backs of the photos. Maybe one of the names would be suitable for their unborn child.

"Eunice, Stella, Sheldon, Bert – um, no," Lori muttered to herself as she continued to look through the documents. It was fascinating to be able to peruse the documents that had shaped her husband's family in so many important ways. Although Lori had never met the people whose names graced the records she was viewing, she certainly felt them near – if only because Chris was a leaf on their family tree. She had no idea just how near some of them were.

She was concentrating so deeply on the task at hand that she didn't hear Hannah pad quietly into the room. Lori started violently when Hannah said, "What are you doing, mommy?"

Clutching a hand to her chest, Lori smiled at Hannah to reassure her. "Sorry, baby, mommy didn't hear you come in. I'm looking through some papers and pictures from your daddy's side of the family. See this?" Lori held up the framed photo of Miner Farm. "This is a picture of our house taken a long, long time ago."

Hannah looked at the vintage photo for a moment, her hazel eyes serious, before nodding. She scanned the surface of the bed, which was covered with all the items her mother had pulled from the box. Suddenly her face lit up and she grabbed for the photo of the young boy and baby girl. "Look mommy, it's Joseph and Emily!"

Lori, uncertain, echoed "Joseph and Emily?" This had to be another example of her daughter's imagination and preoccupation with her imaginary friends. "Do you mean this is how you imagine Joseph and Emily might've looked when they were younger?" Lori remembered that Hannah had described her friends as being four and eight years old.

"No, mommy," Hannah said impatiently "this is Joseph and Emily. I recognize them, and Joseph says the picture was taken when they were younger."

Although Lori's mind was racing, she tried to maintain her calm and smiled slightly. "Really? Wow, Hannah, how special that I finally get to see a picture of your friends. By the way, does your friend, Emily, know what year she was born?"

Hannah seemed to listen for a moment, then said, "Nineteen-oh-eight." Turning, she moved toward the door. "I'm going to play dolls with Emily, okay?"

"Of course Hannah, go ahead." Lori managed to get the words out despite the cold blood pulsing coarsely through her veins. Taking a deep breath, she picked up the photo of the children that Hannah had placed face-up on the bed. Turning it over, she saw a looping script written in black ink, slightly faded by time:

Joseph – 4 years old and two months
Emily – 5 months
December 1908

"It can't be," Lori whispered to herself. She was tempted to pinch herself to make sure she wasn't dreaming, but didn't bother. Yes, she was awake. Yes, Hannah, who'd never seen the photo before and wasn't yet able to read the inscription on the back, had attributed the photo to two children she claimed to see and play with, although her parents had never laid eyes on them. Could they really be sharing their home with the spirits of two of Chris' deceased relatives?

Lori decided to investigate a bit further by looking in the family Bible. She'd never looked through it before, but knew families often kept informal genealogical records in Bibles in the form of handwritten entries. She picked up the volume. It's spine looked fragile, so she took extra care and slowly opened the cover. There were three pages filled with handwritten notations. Two particular entries on the second page leapt out at her:

Joseph Scott Miner - born 1904, died 1912
Emily Margaret Miner – born 1908, died 1912

She didn't know whether to laugh or cry.

Lori closed the Bible and set it down on the bed, lost in thought. She was desperately searching for some way to cast the situation aside as an odd coincidence, wanting to believe that there was some logical explanation. It wasn't that she was afraid of these "ghost children," and she didn't think they'd do any harm; it was just a lot to get her mind around. She was also alarmed to see that both Emily and Joseph had died in the same year. What had happened to them? Lori decided to do a bit more digging in the Miner family documents to see if she could answer the question of how the children had died. Logic-minded Chris was going to want all the details – just as she did.

When the phone rang ten minutes later, Lori ran to answer it, passing Hannah, who was playing quietly in her room – probably with Emily. Lori pressed the on/answer button on the cordless phone and said a breathless hello.

"Hi, Lori, it's me," Chris said, a bit tersely. "I'm sorry, but I'm going to have to stay in the city tonight. We're on a major deadline, preparing for the presentation to our main client, and we just lost data, which has created a gaping hole.

We're going to retrieve the data, and I'll be able to fill it into our presentation, but it's going to be an incredibly long night."

When he paused to breathe, Lori soothingly said, "I understand, honey. Don't worry about us. We'll miss you, but even I know this deadline is set in stone. You'll order some food in, right? You'll need fuel for such an ordeal."

"Yes, there's a big group of us staying, so I'm going to expense a nice dinner – delivery, of course. I don't know if I'll get to sleep, but if I do, the firm will put me up at the Omni Berkshire."

"Okay, well I'll let you get back to it. I've got a lot to tell you, but it's nothing that can't wait until after you're done with this big push. Hannah and I are fine."

"I'll call you later if I get the chance – and thanks for understanding, Lori. I can't wait to see you guys tomorrow! I love you."

"I love you too, Chris. Take care of yourself, sweetie!" Lori said and hung up the phone. She was disappointed he wasn't coming home and knew Hannah would be too, but it gave her a bit more time to dig into the history of the mysterious Miner children. She'd spend more time combing the box's contents for information after she put Hannah to bed that night.

She finally found the missing piece of the puzzle in an old local newspaper that was so brittle and yellowed that Lori was worried it would crumble in her hands. It was dated October 26, 1912, and a story on the front page told of the influenza epidemic that had hit the region, killing dozens – mostly children and the elderly. An inside page revealed the obituaries of those lost in the epidemic, including Emily and Joseph Miner. There was one obituary for both children, and it listed their surviving relatives, including their parents: Margaret and George Miner. As Hannah slept soundly in her bedroom, Lori cried tears of anguish and heartache for Margaret and George, imagining the agony of losing both of their children. The obituary mentioned no surviving siblings. Lori didn't know how a parent survived something like that, but sincerely hoped Margaret and George had managed to find some peace in time.

Lori sighed, stood – a bit slowly – and made her way down the hall to Hannah's room. She wanted to give her another kiss before going bed, all too aware that each day with her child was a gift she couldn't afford to take for granted. She silently said a prayer that Hannah would have a long, happy, and healthy life and wished the same for her unborn son or daughter.

Chris called early the next morning and told her they'd met their deadline – with minutes to spare. He was looking forward to seeing her and Hannah and said he should be in on the five o'clock train; he was cutting out a little early. Lori decided to make another of Chris' favorite meals for dinner: a chicken dish with loads of garlic, mashed potatoes, and sautéed spinach.

Lori and Hannah had some breakfast and then went for a bike ride, flying through the warm summer air. They headed into town and stopped for ice cream before visiting the grocery store and buying a few missing ingredients for dinner. Back at the farm, Hannah said she was going to color in her room while Lori finished putting her purchases away. With all the groceries settled, Lori headed upstairs to check on Hannah. Expecting to see her at her little table in the corner, Lori was surprised to see Hannah in the far corner of her room, prying at one of the floorboards. She'd pulled back the corner of her pink area rug, and was patiently working at one of the dark brown wooden slats with her small fingers. Lori saw it move a bit as if it were already loosened.

"Honey, what are you doing?" Trying to keep her tone light, Lori continued, "Did you drop one of your crayons?"

"No, mommy," Hannah said, "I'm trying to find something for my friends, Emily and Joseph. They said they have a treasure under this board, from when they lived here with their mommy and daddy. They say it's still in there."

Lori crossed to her daughter and knelt beside her. "Here, let me try pulling it up, okay?"

After a wiggle or two, Lori was able to pry up the board and both she and Hannah peered down at the recessed space below, which was approximately two inches wide, six inches long, and two inches deep. Nestled inside was, indeed, an old treasure. Lori reached down and picked up a small metal spoon. It was approximately three and a half inches long, with a curved handle. It was both tarnished and a bit rusty.

"Wow, look, mommy!" Hannah's eyes were shining with excitement. "Emily and Joseph both played with this spoon – a real long time ago, they said. Emily used to pretend to feed her baby dolls with it, and Joseph used it to dig up worms when he and his daddy were going to go fishing at the lake!"

Lori handed the spoon to Hannah, who examined it carefully and held it close as if it was a prized possession. She nearly hugged it, which showed Lori just how much Hannah's invisible friends meant to her. Lori was touched.

"Mommy, they're so happy that we found their spoon. They want me to have it so I can use it when I play with my little brother."

Lori was stunned to hear her daughter's words. The hair on the back of Lori's neck stood on end, but she smiled faintly at her daughter as she said, "But you don't have a little brother, Hannah."

"Emily and Joseph say that there's a baby in your tummy, even though I can't see it yet, and that it's a boy. They say he's a good baby, and my brother and I will have lots of fun playing together – like they do. Are they right? Am I getting a little brother soon?"

If Lori had any lingering doubts about whether or not Hannah was really talking with two spirit children, they were now gone. Lori was awash with emotion and a bit stumped all at once. She wasn't quite sure what to say as she and Chris had planned to wait to tell Hannah about the baby, and wanted to do it together. However, it seemed that the spirit world was moving up the timeline a bit, so Lori took a deep breath and forged ahead.

"Yes, honey, mommy is pregnant. We're going to have a baby in about seven and half months. I know that sounds like a long time to wait, but the time will fly by! Daddy and I just found out a few days ago and, although the test I took didn't say if the baby was a boy or a girl, I'll bet you're going to have a little brother just like Emily and Joseph say."

Hannah bounced excitedly where she sat and squealed, "Hurray! I can't wait for the baby to get here!" She started peppering Lori with questions, and Lori silently wished that Chris were home already – better to share in the fun and insanity of this "unique" situation with her other half.

Later that night, after some of the excitement had subsided and they were all in bed, Lori reflected on the evening. Chris had arrived on the five o'clock train, as promised. She'd pulled her husband aside and told him the story - start to finish - while Hannah watched an episode of SpongeBob SquarePants on TV. Lori presented the story with visual aids, including the cabinet card photo, the Bible, and the newspaper article. Chris had taken it pretty well actually and hadn't seemed particularly alarmed at the idea of having four kids around the house instead of their two.

Lori didn't know if the current living arrangements would continue - whether Joseph and Emily would always be around and would continue to communicate with Hannah. Lori did know that she was grateful to her husband's distant relatives. They'd helped Hannah accept the idea of a soon-to-be sibling with excitement and happiness, and that was a good thing for everyone living at Miner Farm.

An Altered Existence

The Late Bloomer of Bishop

No one in the town of Bishop ever thought Kate Mitchell would get married – including Kate Mitchell herself. Kate was, well, different. For starters, she was nearly as tall as most full-grown men in town by the time she was fourteen years old. She had a plain face that bordered on hostile looking if she wasn't smiling, and she rarely smiled due to an incredibly wide gap between her top two front teeth that made her feel self-conscious. She also had very large, rough hands, prominent ears, and a somewhat deep and rusty voice. In fact, there wasn't much about Kate Mitchell that appeared to be soft, save the modest swell of her breasts and hips. She often thought that if she didn't have those curves, she'd truly be a woman in a man's body.

Over the years she'd tried to count her blessings and focus on the things she did have control of - like her skills, abilities, and work ethic - but those things didn't help much when it came to chemistry and attraction between a man and a woman. Kate suspected her reserved personality and quiet ways were another mark against her, but she was hard pressed to giggle and bat her lashes to help attract a man. Her giggle wasn't feminine sounding at all, and her eyelashes were hardly worth mentioning.

It was some consolation to Kate that the people of Bishop did praise her skills, abilities, and work ethic. She was highly regarded by the ladies for the quality of her "woman's work." They gushed over her exquisite needlework, for Kate was particularly adept at both crocheting and embroidery. They secretly whispered amongst themselves, wondering how on earth she did such fine and detailed work with such big hands. The ladies of Bishop also praised her cooking and baking, and Kate's apple pie won the blue ribbon at the county fair nearly every year. The crust was perfection: buttery, flakey, and golden brown.

The men of Bishop gave Kate grudging respect as well, for she could work as hard as man and was just as capable around a farm. From plowing and planting to working with horses and caring for the other livestock, she could meet a man task for task. Perhaps those strengths, combined with Kate's shooting ability and marksmanship, helped to dim any possible romantic interest that might've grown. The men of Bishop wanted to wear the pants in the family, and they knew Kate was just as comfortable in pants as she was in dresses.

By the age of twenty-two, Kate had resigned herself to life as a single woman. No man had shown her the least bit of interest, so she got on with her life – she was nothing if not practical. By the time she was thirty, she knew for sure that she'd never marry or have children. The secret flame of hope was fully extinguished by then.

Her world changed forever the day she met Henry Collins. She was in the barn shoeing a horse, bent over, with the horse's hoof held on her knee with her left hand, hammering with her right, when she met her future husband. She drove the final nail home in one strike, finishing the shoeing job on the pinto, Rebel, when she heard a deep voice say, "That's a powerful strike you've got there, fella."

Kate was used to being mistaken for a man, especially when she was working on the farm in men's pants, a work shirt, and a wide-brimmed hat. When she straightened and faced the stranger, he quickly realized his mistake. His eyes swept her bosom before quickly moving up to her face. Kate knew he hadn't seen her face when he'd commented, bent down as she was, and decided to forgive his comment. Besides, she'd take compliments where she could get them, and she was proud of her horse-shoeing skills. The tiniest smile crinkled the corner of her eyes, and she ground out a quiet "Thank you."

Henry saw the warmth, restrained as it was, and in that moment he noticed her eyes. Few had ever taken the time to notice their beauty, given the coarse exterior that housed them, but Kate's eyes were lovely - a rich brown with flecks of gold that plainly showed her intelligence and sense of humor. Henry felt a spark of intrigue. He was out at the Mitchell family farm to see about a horse and started chatting with Kate. He explained that he was new in town and began the slow process of drawing her out of her thick shell. So began his courtship of the old maid, Kate Mitchell.

Henry sensed Kate would be resistant to his attention and decided he'd have to wear her down a bit simply by spending a lot of time with her, becoming familiar and safe to her. Henry was, indeed, a safe man: kind, warm-hearted, and attentive. In fact, it was his attention to the details of Kate that changed his intrigue to love and attraction.

Kate wasn't soft in the expected ways, like in her appearance or speech, but she was so very tender in a hundred tiny ways. As Henry spent time with her, he saw all the facets of her that no one had ever taken time to notice. She loved sitting outside to watch the sun set and stayed out until the stars began twinkling in the night sky. She adored pansies and kept a small bunch in a glass jar on the kitchen table – perhaps the most overtly feminine display on Kate's part. She also loved birds and listening to their calls; whenever she found a bird feather, she'd pick it up and add it to her collection. She went to church regularly and - although she didn't spend her free time reading the Bible, like some of the women in Bishop – Henry knew she practiced the lessons within its pages. She was quietly charitable and helpful, wanting neither praise nor thanks. She simply wanted to lend a hand to those in need. Henry saw all the little pieces of Kate and assembled them in his heart. He knew that she was the quintessential diamond in the rough. His Kate was a piece of solid gold waiting in the depths of a murky river, waiting for someone to reveal her luster.

When Henry Collins proposed to Kate Mitchell, she paused, wondering how she'd gone from an old maid to someone's fiancée with essentially no effort on her part. In the end, she decided it didn't matter. She knew she was blessed. Henry was a very loveable man – as open, friendly, and relaxed as she was reserved and restrained. She knew this proposal would set tongues to wagging in town and that folks would likely call them an odd couple, but Kate didn't care. She was loved, and she accepted Henry's proposal with joy in her heart and a twinkle in her eye.

Henry and Kate Collins settled into a happy life. They were hoping to have children, but none came, so they continued on as they were, living, loving, and working together. The division of labor was relatively traditional, with Kate taking care of more of the indoor work like cooking, cleaning, mending, and washing while Henry tended the livestock and farmed. However, Henry often helped Kate with "women's duties" like washing clothes in the huge pot over the fire outside and took on dinner duty from time to time so she'd have a break from cooking. Likewise, Kate would help him with the animals, including birthing calves and foals and the construction of outbuildings on their property.

Henry was an incredible craftsman and had a separate workshop dedicated to his woodworking. He made wooden tables, chairs, cradles, and rocking chairs that brought in additional income. Whenever Kate had a moment to spare from her own work, she loved to watch Henry working in his shop and greatly admired his ability to create pieces of such beauty and durability. She was particularly fond of the cradles and so wished they'd had need to keep one for themselves. Yet she never kept the thought in her head for long as she already felt like the luckiest woman alive to have been gifted with her beloved Henry.

Although they seldom spoke of children now that they were nearly forty and seemed unlikely to conceive, Henry knew Kate was silently yearning for a child. One day a peddler passed by the farm in his wagon, and he had a young canary in a cage. The bird was more of a pet than it was merchandise, but Henry convinced the man to sell the bird to him. Kate would love the bird, with its beautiful and intricate songs; Henry knew the canary was no substitute for the child they really wanted, yet he hoped to bring a bit more joy into Kate's life. Henry presented the bird to her immediately, and Kate was thrilled with the delicate little creature. They named the bird Sunny and hung his cage near the kitchen table so he'd be nearby as Kate worked in the kitchen.

Kate adored Sunny, who added so much to their little family. His songs were a treat, and he always burst into song when Henry came into the room. Kate, being on the quiet side, wasn't known for laughing overly much, but Sunny's antics during his bath time always stole a chuckle or two from her. She often told Henry that she had no idea how something so small could make such a big, watery mess, splashing and preening the way he did. It was clear she didn't mind mopping things up though, not in the least. Sunny became interwoven into their daily lives: Where they had been two, now they were three.

One morning, Henry returned to the house just after dawn, having milked the cows and fed all the livestock. Kate usually had breakfast cooking by this time, nearly on the table, so Henry was struck by the silence as he entered. Alarmed, Henry turned into the kitchen and spied Kate in the rocking chair they'd placed in the very corner of the room, near Sunny's cage. What he saw shocked him to the core.

In the twelve years they'd been married, Henry had never seen his wife cry, not even when a horse they were shoeing managed to kick her and nearly broke her leg. Now Kate was sitting absolutely still in the rocking chair, tears streaming down her face.

"Kate, what's wrong?" Henry asked, his extreme concern clearly written on his face.

He hadn't noticed the position of her hands, cupped together in her lap, and she silently parted them to reveal Sunny, who was laying on his back, feet up and stiff. Kate looked down at her beloved pet, and some of her tears fell on his glossy feathers. In the instant it took for Henry to cross to Kate, her chest started to visibly heave and her voice broke. The audible sobs burst forth like a dam overflowing. Henry wrapped both Kate and the late Sunny in an embrace. It nearly broke Henry's heart to hear Kate cry that way; all he could think to do was hold her even tighter and whisper to her to let all the tears out.

When her sobs had subsided to a hiccupping staccato, Henry gently lifted Sunny from Kate's hands and placed the bird on a clean tea towel. He dried his wife's eyes with his handkerchief and had her blow her nose. Henry then guided Kate to their bed, urged her to lie down, and gently laid a blanket over her. He stayed with her, lightly stroking her hair, until she closed her eyes and finally drifted off to sleep.

While Kate rested, Henry quickly crafted a small wooden box - a coffin of sorts - for little Sunny. He lined the box with a scrap of velvet he had left over from making Kate a jewelry box and then gathered flowers. By the time Kate roused herself from her nap, Henry had Sunny lying in repose on their sideboard – his tiny coffin surrounded by the fresh flowers and flanked by two burning candles. Tears welled up in her eyes again to see Sunny and the care Henry had put into the preparations.

"Oh, Henry, thank you," Kate hoarsely whispered. She tried to swallow the lump in her throat before speaking again, but it wouldn't go anywhere, so she spoke around it instead. "I think he'd like to be buried under the oak tree, don't you?"

"Kate, I think Sunny would love that – what a wonderful suggestion," Henry said. Each word he spoke was a tender offering to his wife and her wounded heart.

After they buried their beloved pet beneath the oak tree, Henry cooked up some breakfast. He served Kate a cup of hot tea and made her eat some eggs and toast, although she said she wasn't hungry. In the end, she ate what he served because she knew it would please him and that he was already very worried about her.

From the day Sunny died Kate kept one of his tiny yellow and white feathers in a gold locket she wore hanging beneath her clothes. On one side she had a picture of Henry, and on the other she kept the feather. But life went on, and they continued as they had been, living, loving, and working together.

The first earth-shattering change in Kate's life had been being "found" and wooed by her beloved husband, Henry. The second earth-shattering change in Kate's life came compliments of the fifteen-year-old girl who knocked on their front door in the dead of night. Hearing the faint yet insistent knock, Henry lit a lantern and grabbed the pistol from his nightstand. He and Kate carefully opened the door, ready for anything. They found a wild-eyed stranger drenched in sweat, with both hands pressed against her hugely pregnant belly. The girl managed to spit out "Please help me, the baby's coming now!" before howling with the pain of another contraction. Clearly there was no time to summon a doctor or midwife, so Kate and Henry did what they'd done together dozens of times on the farm: They helped birth a baby. This time the new arrival just happened to be human.

The baby announced its arrival into the world with a triumphant cry, and Kate and Henry smiled at each other as they marveled over the newly born baby. "It's a girl!" Kate said. They held the baby out to the young mother, who had told them her name was Peggy as they settled her on the guest room bed for the delivery, but she didn't reach to take her child. "I'm so tired. Can I just rest a bit before I hold her?" Of course she could rest, they said, and they helped her settle in to sleep.

Peggy dozed while Kate cleaned and cared for the baby. Kate wrapped the child in a blanket she'd crocheted and, during her ministrations, Henry came into the room with one of the handmade cradles he'd crafted in his woodshop. He also brought in a rocking chair and set it next to the cradle. Kate sat in the chair and rocked the baby girl while Henry stood beside them both, looking down with a soft smile. They were so wrapped up in the sight of the newborn that they didn't notice that Peggy had opened her eyes and was watching them intently.

Kate and Henry stayed in the room a while, making sure their two guests were comfortable before finally going to bed themselves. It was nearly dawn by the time they lay down to sleep.

Kate and Henry woke with a start when they heard the baby cry a few hours later. Kate hurried to the guest room to help and was bewildered to find Peggy missing. She had Henry check around the house, thinking that perhaps the girl had risen and was looking for something she needed for herself or the baby. Kate called to Henry "Have you checked the outhouse, just in case she went to empty her chamber pot?"

Henry entered the room holding a sheet of paper, which he was still reading. "She's gone." He had to speak up to be heard over the continuing cries of the hungry infant. "She says she's so sorry for any trouble she's caused and for leaving us with the baby, but she can't keep her. It seems Peggy is unmarried, has no money, and has no family to help her. She said she can see our home is a happy one and that it's as clear as day that we want a child of our own. She hopes we'll keep this little one and raise her as our daughter."

Husband and wife looked at each other in utter shock, then hugged each other in fierce joy. They had a chance to raise a child, forty-somethings that they were, and they meant to do just that.

The folks in the town of Bishop all agreed: The baby girl, whom Kate and Henry named Isabel, softened Kate's demeanor quite a bit. In the past, she'd felt out of place and awkward and had built walls to keep those feelings at bay. She had to overcome her shyness rather quickly as she got a crash course in motherhood. She now smiled with little reservation and actually socialized with the ladies of the town for the first time.

The town rallied behind them and held an impromptu baby shower for the new parents. The adoption of Isabel Catherine Collins was soon official, and Henry, Kate, and Isabel were a real family. The love Kate and Henry had shared as two increased tenfold as they welcomed an utterly unexpected daughter.

Henry smiled to see Kate in her rocking chair in the corner of the kitchen. She smiled and cooed at the baby, gently rocking back and forth. Seeing that Henry was about to leave the room to do the evening's milking, Kate gave him a smile that had a new depth to it. Their love had been strong and full before Isabel's arrival; this new dimension was just an added bonus.

Henry walked toward the back door, but he paused at their maple and glass curio cabinet. His eyes were drawn to the first of two portraits he and Kate had taken, from approximately three years ago. Henry sat while Kate stood, with her right arm on his left shoulder. Looking at the photo, Henry acknowledged that Kate looked quite stern, although she was always lovely to him.

The more recent portrait depicted the changes in both his wife and their family. Kate and Henry both sat in chairs, turned slightly toward each other with their knees nearly touching. Isabel was tucked firmly into the crook of Kate's left arm, and a mild but joyous smile playing about Kate's mouth, crinkling the corner of her eyes. Kate's right had was firmly grasped in Henry's, joining them as husband and wife and as a family.

Each Passing Moment

Tick tock tick tock!

The very sounds that used to be so welcome, guiding Alan Hamilton comfortably through each and every day, now created a completely different feeling within him. He stared down at his pocket watch, opened to reveal the ornate face, and tried to quell the panic that was rising within him.

Tick tock tick tock!

It had been a full ten minutes since Alan had been notified of a complication during his wife's labor and delivery and that she'd lost a dangerous amount of blood. Both mother and child were in jeopardy. In the minutes that had followed, Alan experienced his first anxiety attack.

Tick tock tick tock!

Alan Hamilton was not used to feeling out of control. He was used to having tight control over his universe. He lived by the watch – by the clock, by the time of day - and had a precise routine. One might attribute this to his childhood, for he grew up in a Catholic orphanage in which the nuns ran a tight ship. Everything that took place during Alan's childhood was strictly ordered and scheduled: his waking time, breakfast, how many minutes he was allowed to play outside - everything. Some of the children resisted this structure, but Alan thrived on structure. He was the tidiest and most punctual child in the orphanage, even going beyond the nuns' requirements by alphabetizing his few books, grouping all clothing by color, and neatly aligning his comb and toothbrush so they were vertically presented and exactly one inch from each other.

Tick tock tick tock!

The only thing Alan did that was remotely out of the nuns' expectations or schedule was to disassemble things so he could see how they worked. Amazingly, he was always able to reassemble them perfectly and never had any extra parts left over. Initially, the sisters were aghast at this behavior, but eventually they chalked it up to his curious mind and let him do as he wished - once they were certain his ministrations would have no ill effects on the items in question.

Tick tock tick tock!

When Alan left the orphanage after finishing secondary school, he was lucky enough to become an apprentice in the field that suited him best: watch making. This trade required qualities that Alan had in spades: mechanical precision, patience, logical thought, and innovation. Alan was always immaculately cleaned and groomed, and his workstation consistently reflected the same quality, with no tools ever out of place. No oil smudged the work surface, no gears were strewn carelessly about. In fact, members of the guild noticed he was almost too clean, washing his hands often and replacing a tool immediately after he'd used it. Yet he was an excellent worker and was completely devoted to the field, so they overlooked what could've been deemed mildly obsessive behavior.

Tick tock tick tock!

Following his apprenticeship, Alan was invited to join a partnership, and was soon wrapped up in a thriving business. He continued to excel at his craft. He was able to purchase a modest, yet lovely home, in which everything was clean and kept in its place. Alan's house was a mere ten-minute walk from his workshop and store, and he walked along at a brisk pace, never allowing himself to dawdle. *Tick tock tick tock.* He loved the sound of his heels striking the cobblestone walkways as he traveled along the streets.

Tick tock tick tock!

Alan's structure, discipline, order, and what some would call rigidity led those who knew him to question if he was, in fact, part machine. Was he made of flesh and bone, heart and soul, or was he composed of the very components that he built into his watches and other timekeeping devices? Alan Hamilton was a handsome man, but he was most certainly closed off. Although he was a good and honest man, he was without true connections of the heart. Being an orphan undoubtedly influenced and fostered Alan's detachment, but he wasn't even aware there was a problem. He didn't realize his one-track mind, always focused on watch making and horology, was off-putting to the general public. This was precisely why Alan, a handsome and successful career man, went home to a silent and perfectly ordered home every night, having no one to share his life with.

Tick tock tick tock!

Alan's biggest aspiration, aside from what he was already achieving as a watchmaker and business partner, was to be president. Not president of the country, but rather president of the local Horology Society. Horology, the study of the science and art of timekeeping devices, consumed Alan Hamilton – as did the idea of being president. He wanted to be the youngest president the society had ever had and was certainly well qualified for the post. Yet elections to such posts are often political instead of merit based, as anyone with life experience knew, and the Horology Society was no different. This was how Alan Hamilton married Beth Harding – a woman he barely knew – in her family's church.

Tick tock tick tock!

Alan's marriage to Beth Harding was an almost immediate path to the presidency he so craved, based on the alliances he'd forge with her father, and so Alan had agreed to wed the twenty-eight-year-old Beth after meeting her at a dinner party to which her parents had invited him. Naturally the couple didn't rush off to the church the very next day, but the brief courtship did start that very night, after Alan had a discussion with his future father-in-law behind closed study doors.

Tick tock tick tock!

Alan saw the marriage as a logical progression in his life. He'd secured a career and purchased a home; moving on to marriage and children was the next logical step. He almost saw his marriage as something to check off his list, but he was also hoping for a loving companion. He didn't expect to be in love with Beth, nor did he expect her to be in love with him, but he felt certain their marriage could be built upon respect for each other and common goals. Many marriages had been business arrangements throughout history. Why shouldn't Alan and Beth make a similar arrangement if it benefited them both?

Tick tock tick tock!

Despite being raised in a Catholic orphanage, Alan Hamilton was not religious. He believed in science. He wasn't intolerant, however, and did not begrudge his fiancée's family the satisfaction of seeing the lovely Beth married in the same church in which she had been christened. The newlyweds began their lives together as Mr. and Mrs. Alan Hamilton. Although Beth didn't walk to a rhythmic *tick tock tick tock*, she was - thankfully - very tidy.

Tick tock tick tock!

Soon happily ensconced in his first term as the Horology Society president, Alan was initially a tepid spouse. Beth sensed his detachment and, luckily, refused to take it personally. She'd gone into the marriage with open eyes, knowing their union was an arrangement that served both their purposes. She was tired of being called an old maid and, although they were kind and well meaning, she was desperate to get out of her parents' home. She knew it was unlikely that Alan would change, but she still began a campaign to personalize their marriage – to stir something in him that wasn't mechanically based. She would've preferred to know her husband much more intimately, emotionally, before they conceived their first child, yet that was not to be. As the weeks passed and her monthly flow did not come, it became clear that Beth Hamilton was pregnant.

Tick tock tick tock!

When Beth told Alan the news, he said all the right things. He was so happy and was looking forward to meeting their son or daughter. The following day he gave Beth a beautiful pendant watch to commemorate the occasion. As the months passed, they grew closer while working together on the baby's nursery, discussing possible names, and sharing stories from their own childhoods.

"My favorite memory of my father is the time he played blocks with me," Beth said. "I was usually with my mother or the nanny. Father seldom spent time with me unless it was at mealtimes or some other family event. On this particular day, he sat with me on the floor and helped me build a tall castle out of blocks, and I remember us laughing when the structure finally crumbled. How I wish we'd spent more time together, just the two of us." Beth gazed off into the distance, eyes slightly unfocused. It was that statement that made Alan begin to ponder what kind of father he wanted to be.

Tick tock tick tock!

Alan still stared frantically at his open watch, blind to any real sense of time. The man who was ruled by order, calm, reason, and precision finally realized how wildly his life had spun out of its usual orbit. He acknowledged that, although he was tightly wound, he had no real control over what was happening around him. The woman he'd married for logical reasons, who was bearing his child – the most complex and amazing thing he could ever hope to co-create – could be dying in the other room while he sat hopelessly in a chair in the nearly silent waiting room.

Tick tock tick tock!
Tick tock tick tock!
Tick tock tick tock!

The ticks and tocks that had been his constant companion since he'd begun his apprenticeship now faded away. Stress and anxiety filled Alan's ears with the sound of his own frantic blood flow. His heart beat as rapidly as the wings of a hummingbird, and he felt as frail as one of those tiny, winged, jewel-like creatures when he realized how deeply he cared. Alan loved Beth and their child. His hands went numb at the thought of losing one or both of them. His watch fell to the ground. He automatically bent to pick it up without noticing that the crystal covering the face was scratched and cracked.

As he straightened to continue his tense vigil, the doctor approached. "Mr. Hamilton, both mother and child are safe and are resting comfortably. You may see them now."

Bug-eyed and nearly choked with relief, Alan followed the doctor down the hall, his Adam's apple bobbing furiously as he struggled to regain his composure. Gone was the *tick tock tick tock* – it had been replaced by the thudding of his own heart as he entered Beth's room and saw her with a tightly wrapped bundle in her arms. She looked pale and was clearly exhausted, but Beth gave her husband a valiant and warm smile as he approached. Alan felt as though his heart might burst as he looked down upon them.

"Congratulations, you're a father. Meet your baby girl," Beth said softly to Alan.

Alan managed a slightly gruff "Hello there, little one. I'm your Papa, and I love you very much!"

Beth looked at him and recognized how present and focused he was, how earnest and caring. She knew the transformation that slowly emerged when she announced her pregnancy to Alan had taken another huge leap forward. She knew he was now completely invested in their marriage – in their family.

Sighing contentedly, she relaxed back into the pillows. She smiled again and nearly melted when her husband said – and clearly meant – "I love you, too, Beth. I love you more and more with each passing moment."

The Tattooed Lady

"Hurry, Francesca, we're nearly there!" Anthony cried as they wove their way through the crowds to the most scandalous sideshow at the circus – at least according to their mother. Their father, who was extremely hen pecked, never had much to say on the matter. However, their mother had made it exceedingly clear that they were to stay far away from the Tattooed Lady and the Tattooed Man – people simply covered in tattoos. Naturally that was the one thing that twins Anthony and Francesca wanted to see.

Mother thought these "show folk" were vile, corrupted people of the underworld – especially the woman. Why else would she agree to appear in public, before hundreds of strangers, with her arms and legs completely exposed? Mother also suspected that these tattooed people might worship the devil, though she had no hard evidence. The twins had taken their allotted spending money from their parents and promised to stay away from the sideshows and other "unsavory" things, but their fingers had been crossed behind their backs as they promised. They felt sorry for fibbing, but they had to see this one particular show.

When they finally reached the sideshow in question, they weren't disappointed. As promised, virtually every inch of the man and woman on display was covered in ink – save their faces, hands, and necks. Eyes wide, Francesca and Anthony looked at each other, grins on their faces, before turning back to the front of the exhibit – craning to hear every word that came out of the barker's mouth. They stood, entranced, until the show finally concluded.

Instead of heading off to find their parents, they stood whispering to themselves, deciding to try and talk to the two stars of the show. They crept back behind the curtain and saw the man and woman sitting in chairs against the tent's back walls. They were both smoking cigarettes and sipping soda from bottles. Nothing too scandalous so far. Surely it would be okay to ask them a few questions, provided they were receptive! The children were ready to bolt should someone start yelling that they didn't belong back there, but they were emboldened by their raging curiosities.

Anthony took charge by clearing his throat and saying, "Excuse me, ma'am, sir. May we ask you some questions?"

The inked pair turned toward the sound of Anthony's attempt at polite bravery and smiled. "Sure, come on over." The Tattooed Lady gestured them over to two of the extra chairs opposite them, and she and the Tattooed Man stubbed out their cigarettes on the dirt floor.

Hardly believing their luck, Francesca and Anthony scurried over and sat, Francesca across from the lady and Anthony across from the man. The foursome made introductions as if they were enjoying an afternoon tea party instead of a sideshow question-and-answer session.

The Tattooed Lady's name was Ella Stevenson. The Tattooed Man's name was Herbert Stevenson – but his friends called him Herb. He invited the children to call him Herb right off the bat. Ella and Herb said they'd been married for ten years and lived their lives together on the road. They could see their young guests were nearly about to burst from holding their questions in and urged them to go ahead and start asking.

"Does it hurt to get tattooed?" Francesca asked.

"Yes, it does hurt. Some people tolerate pain better than others, and I know some people wouldn't like it at all, but Herb and I do just fine getting tattooed. We think the pain is worth it because when the tattoo artist is done, we're left with a lovely keepsake that we'll always have." Ella pointed to a morning glory blooming on her left forearm – the vine wrapped around her wrist – and the twins eyed it seriously.

Anthony was next. "Why do you have so many tattoos?"

Herb chuckled and said, "I just started with one, never imagining I'd end up covered! I really liked that first one though, so I kept adding to my collection. Then I found out I could make a good living by being the tattooed man in the circus and added several more so I'd qualify for the job. That's about the time I met Ella."

"Once Herb and I married, it made sense that I'd get tattooed as well and be his tattooed lady. I earn a good salary too, so we're in fine shape between circus tours. Plus, we get to travel and meet all kinds of interesting people. Like you two, for example." Ella spoke sincerely, without a hint of the condescension usually adopted by adults speaking to children.

Anthony and Francesca exchanged a quick glance, read each other's faces as clearly as if they'd spoken. *What a fascinating life!*

"Which tattoo is your favorite?" Francesca shyly put to Ella. Ella stood, turned, and pointed to a heart on her upper back, which featured her and Herb's names intertwined. Their portraits, rendered in black and white, flanked their names – portraits that had been captured some years before. Mrs. and Mrs. Stevenson looked to be in their late thirties and, although the children continued to pepper them with questions about their ink, they were too polite to ask them their ages.

"How long did that tattoo take?" queried Anthony, pointing to a newly inked bird on her right forearm. Ella answered that it took a few hours. She explained that it would've taken much longer if the tattoo had been applied the old fashioned way – piecing the skin one prick at a time with a handheld needle (sometimes attached to a stick) or sharpened stick dipped in ink. Edison's invention of the electric pen, modified a bit and outfitted with ink, sped the process up quite a bit. It also resulted in more detailed tattoos, which the Stevensons preferred. They showed the children examples of tattoos done with the old method, and then pointed out the "electric pen" work. The twins appreciated the noticeable difference.

Anthony directed his next question to Herb in a "man-to-man" manner. "How old were you when you got your first tattoo, Herb?"

Herb pointed to an eagle on his right shoulder and said he'd gotten it on his seventeenth birthday. Francesca popped in with a solemn, "Did it make you cry, Herb?" which made Herb smile. He told the little girl that he didn't cry, but he might've said a curse word or two during the process. The children giggled.

Francesca and Anthony's ears pricked up when they heard their mother calling their names in the distance – several yards from where they sat sequestered in the tent with two of the circus stars. They looked at each other, panicked, and jumped up from their seats. They hastily thanked the hospitable Mr. and Mrs. Stevenson and offered the couple their small hands to shake. Further charmed by the well-mannered children, Ella and Herb shook their hands warmly. When the twins ducked under the side of the tent Herb held up for them, he winked and told the two of them "Good luck!"

Brother and sister ran away from the tattoo side show at full tilt, knowing there would be hell to pay if their mother found them anywhere near it. They ran into their father in front of the animal exhibit and, distracted as he was, he didn't notice from which direction they'd come. Turning, he said, "Oh, there you are. Let's find your mother so we can go home. It's been a long evening, and we've got church in the morning."

Francesca and Anthony tried awfully hard to keep quiet on the way home so they wouldn't spill details of their adventure and get punished. After they'd been put to bed that night, Francesca snuck into Anthony's room, where they spent hours discussing every detail of their evening in matching whispers. The twins agreed that Mr. and Mrs. Stevenson were quite nice and had been so welcoming. Mother had to be wrong, they agreed. It was impossible to believe that Ella or Herb would have anything to do with the devil!

That very night, with silvery moonlight spilling in the bedroom window and pooling dimly onto the floor where Anthony and Francesca sat, they made a momentous decision. They vowed they would each get a tattoo. They'd go together, of course, and they'd get them on their seventeenth birthdays – just like their new friend, Herb. They weren't sure which designs they'd select for their first tattoos, but figured they had years to figure it out. A little more than ten years, to be exact, since they'd turn seven within the month. They also decided they'd practice covering their bodies with tattoos. They'd pool their resources and buy a bottle of India ink as a first step.

Francesca and Anthony purchased the black ink in order to tattoo themselves for the photographic portrait they were going to have taken. Mother had made the appointment and had already picked out their outfits. Francesca was going to wear a light cotton dress with cap sleeves and a skirt that went down to her knees. Anthony was going to wear short pants and a short-sleeved shirt with a bow tie – also cotton. Their outfits left plenty of "canvas" for the twins to work with – namely, their exposed arms and legs.

The night before the portrait appointment was a very busy one. Once their parents were in bed, the children used their black India ink and pens with metal nibs to apply their "tattoos." Anthony drew stars, a bow and arrows, kites, oceans, anchors, birds, and trees on his body while Francesca was partial to flowers, hearts, birds, butterflies, stars, and a crescent moon.

It took hours of painstaking work, but they were finally done. By this time the twins were drooping-eyed exhausted, but were careful to let all the ink dry before dropping off to sleep. They were worried about their mother's reaction, but counted on her changing her mind about tattoos when she saw how well theirs turned out - when she saw all their creativity and hard work laid out on their skin.

The twins severely misjudged how their mother would react. They'd both fallen asleep on Francesca's bed and were jolted awake by their mother's blood-curdling screams. "Oh my God! What have you children done?! How could you? After all your father and I do for you, you defy us in this way and throw the work of the devil in our faces? Bring it into our very home?! How can I possibly take you to have your pictures taken, you ungrateful wretches? I'll be a laughingstock! I can hear it now. 'Look, there goes Mrs. Abbruzzo with her heathen children!' Holy Mary, Mother of God, what did I do to deserve such behavior from my very own flesh and blood?"

Their father, drawn by his wife's banshee cries, simply looked on from the doorway. Francesca and Anthony could've sworn he was suppressing a smile, but they couldn't be sure. Their mother once again commanded their attention, especially when she yanked them both up by the arms and dragged them roughly off the bed.

Pausing her tirade for a moment, she assessed the damage and made a decision. "You will still have your picture taken today, so help me," she hissed. "But you will not display any of this mess! Not one line of ink will be visible in the photo, and when we get home from our appointment I am going to scrub you and whip you within an inch of your life! Our appointment is in an hour, so hurry and get dressed!"

Anthony and Francesca ended up having their pictures taken in full-coverage winter clothing, although it was nearly ninety degrees outside. The other families at the photographic studio looked at them oddly; they were clearly out of season and very much out of place. Francesca's outfit included a crucifix - a belated attempt by their devout mother to ward off evil and sin. The twins were mournful, thinking of the beautiful designs hidden by the woolen stockings, jackets, and other garments. When the photo was snapped, the children looked distant and distracted, with their thwarted plans and the promise of a whipping filling their heads.

Their mother made good on her promise, whipping their backsides with a switch, fiendishly driven on by her anger until even her timid husband said "Enough, Maria," snatching the switch from her hand. Next came the scalding hot water and the scrubbing, which further intensified their pain and left their skin both red and raw. Although their plan had gone horribly wrong and they paid a dear price, they were steadfast in their decisions to get their tattoos when they turned seventeen.

"I don't care if I have to run away from home, I will get my tattoo – I might even get two!" said a petulant and determined Francesca.

"Me too," said Anthony. "All we need is each other." With that, Anthony – the older twin by two minutes – gathered his sister's hand in his. They both fell asleep on Francesca's bed again, although this time the India ink was just a faint memory on their tenderized skin.

Francesca's tears were blinding prisms that caught the sunlight as they spilled from her eyes. As her brother Anthony's coffin was lowered into the parched and brittle soil, she felt as if she'd already cried enough to quench the drought-ravaged earth, yet her supply of tears wasn't even close to being staunched. She'd lost the person closest to her – her fraternal twin and her very best friend. His death had been a freak accident – one that left Francesca solitary and empty. Anthony had been thrown from a horse that spooked when a large tree branch cracked and fell, breaking her twin's neck. He had died instantly. Next to her, her parents voiced their grief with huge, wracking sobs. In the midst of such a surreal scene, Francesca couldn't help but remember that she'd now be alone when she got her first tattoo on her seventeenth birthday.

Every time she thought back to her loss, she felt simultaneously sick and adrift. She tried not to think about it, albeit with varying degrees of success. Since Anthony's death, each year on their birthday, Francesca felt as if she had been split in two. Part of her tried to be happy, celebrating her birthday with her parents. They really did try extra hard to make her birthdays nice, knowing how deeply she mourned and missed Anthony. They even stayed silent when they saw Francesca appear at breakfast the day after each birthday, wearing long sleeves and stockings, her eyes red rimmed. If they knew she stayed up on those birthday nights covering her skin in India ink in memory of her lost twin, they didn't say. They knew they owed her that much.

Francesca's seventeenth birthday was bittersweet. She got the tattoo she'd planned on for so long, but it was a hollow victory without her twin brother at her side. In the end, Francesca combined symbols favored by each twin to form one design. It was oval shaped, with *Francesca & Anthony* in script in the center. The bottom of the design was cupped by Anthony's ocean and curling waves while the top was arced with Francesca's night sky, complete with crescent moon and stars.

As Francesca sat in the tattoo artist's chair, her left upper arm exposed and the tattoo partially complete, she said aloud to her twin, "Herb was right, Anthony. It's painful, but it will be worth it in the end."

A Restless Heart

Sadie McNamara sighed as she put the final details on Candace Jones' veil. If she had to outfit one more bride with a trousseau and wedding attire she might scream. To be surrounded by the very items she herself had longed to wear, day in and day out, was a cruel twist of fate. Here she was, a vibrant woman in her early forties, and she'd never worn the wedding dress she'd designed and handmade so many years ago. True, she'd gotten ahead of herself by creating a gown when she wasn't even engaged, but Sadie had thought she was just being proactive; she'd thought that surely it was just a matter of time before she too would wed. Besides, sewing and designing were like second nature, and the task had kept her busy during some slow hours in the shop.

Sadie was quite pleased with herself for building and running a successful business. Her shop provided the residents of Salvation with sewing materials like basic fabric and thread as well as fine trims like velvet ribbons, fancy fabric flowers, and sparkling beads. She sold the materials that the women of Salvation needed to make their own garments. She also sold some pre-made and finished pieces.

Another part of her thriving business was made-to-order garments. McNamara's Finishings & Finery was the most popular store in the entire county for outfitting young women from well-to-do families with their trousseaus. Sadie custom made chemises, petticoats, slips, nightgowns, and other items the bride would need in her new life. She also created the wedding dress and veil. Some brides ordered traveling suits for their honeymoon as well, although it certainly depended on their budget.

Looking down at the garment she was now working on, a modest but beautiful nightgown of the softest white cotton, Sadie sighed. For just a moment she indulged the envy that was threatening to escape the confines of her heart. She wished she had someone to cuddle into bed with, to intertwine limbs with – a man who'd compliment her on the fine design and construction of her nightgown before enticing her to take it off so they could share the warm pleasure that came from physical contact. Sadie wasn't sure why she was without these moments – what led Candace Jones and others to husbands while she remained without - but she had to admit that it vexed her.

The bells on the door tinkled brightly, drawing Sadie's attention away from the nightgown edged with pale pink ribbon. Men seldom came into her store, so Sadie was a bit startled to see a tall man approaching the counter. She set her work aside, and said, "Good afternoon, sir. May I help you?"

One glance into the stranger's face told Sadie that he was new to Salvation. Unlike most of the lily-white residents of the town, who often burned to a combination of tan and ruddy red, the stranger was olive-skinned, with deep hazel-green eyes flecked with gold. He was neat and clean enough, but Sadie could tell he'd been on the road a while – that his tan was partially from his heritage and partially from many hours in the sun.

Removing his slightly dusty hat from his head, the stranger said, "Can you please direct me to the needles and thread?"

Sadie couldn't quite place his accent, but enjoyed the musical lilt to his voice. It warmed her to the core. Perhaps it was his voice, combined with the intensity in his gorgeous eyes - and his slim but powerful build and broad hands. Sadie finally realized she'd been staring distractedly and that the customer was waiting for a response.

"Oh yes, certainly. I've got quite a selection of both needles and thread, right over here, sir." Sadie gestured weakly to her left, and the stranger followed with his eyes.

As she walked over to the display containing the packets of needles and spools of thread, he smiled slightly, trying to hide his amusement. He didn't want to let on that he was aware of her fascinated gaze. "I'm looking for sturdy needles and thick thread that can patch tears in the canvas covering of my wagon. Our group travels quite a bit, and I need to make some repairs before we leave town later this week. I'd also like some needles and thread that will work for mending clothing." He smiled at Sadie, and she burned brightly, as if she'd been lit from within.

She scolded herself silently while selecting the different types of needles and threads he'd need. *For heaven's sake, Sadie Marie McNamara, you're acting like a love-struck school girl, not a grown woman. A man can't walk into the store without you melting into a puddle of longing? Really!*

She showed the stranger the items he'd need, and he nodded his assent. "Is there anything else I can help you with today, sir?"

"Well, that's all I need in the way of notions, but I wouldn't mind talking with you about the town and the county, if you have a moment or two free. Only if it's convenient though - I don't want to keep you from your work. Perhaps the shop's owner will be angry if you dally, talking to strange men." The mischievous gleam in his eye dared her to take a chance.

"Well, sir, I don't think the owner would mind at all. I'm the owner of this shop, and I'll chat with whomever I like," she said, wrapping up his purchases. "I don't generally talk with strange men, but if you'd be so kind as to introduce yourself, we'll no longer be strangers." Sadie was shocked by the forward and somewhat sassy words coming out of her mouth. Who was she becoming under the influence of this intriguing stranger? She indicated the total on the sales slip she'd quickly written up.

He placed exact change on the counter. "So you're the proprietress of McNamara's Finishings & Finery? Well, in that case, I'm Uriah Smith. It's a pleasure to meet you, Mrs. …?"

"It's Miss, actually. Miss Sadie Marie McNamara." Sadie was tempted to hold her hand out for him to kiss, but she didn't want to seem ridiculous or be rebuffed, so she tucked her hands into the decorative shop apron she wore over her dress.

Uriah, sensing her uncertainty, issued a truncated bow, and said, "Pleased to meet you, Miss Sadie Marie McNamara. What a lovely name. Have you lived in Salvation long?"

"All my life, Mr. Smith. My family is one of the founding families of Salvation, and most of the McNamaras have stayed put. There are a veritable slew of us here in town. If you head down to the barbershop or the blacksmith, you'll meet two of my brothers, Sean and Phillip. There are more McNamaras scattered about, naturally, but they're two that have businesses on this main strip in town. My parents used to own the newspaper, until they sold it to the Carter family."

"I see. You're a local girl with roots that run deep in Salvation. Have you done much traveling?" Uriah eyed Sadie curiously. He wasn't sure how anyone could handle living in one place for so long, staying in the same spot day after day after day.

"I've always longed to travel, but haven't made it out of the state yet. Most of our relatives are here in the county, and since I opened up my shop, there hasn't been much time to travel. I mind the store myself, most of the time, and I've been blessed with a steady flow of business since day one. And you, Mr. Smith? Have you done much traveling?"

"Please, call me Uriah."

"I'd be happy to, Uriah, if you'll call me Sadie."

"Certainly, Sadie. I've done quite a bit of traveling, actually. My family is a bit nomadic, you see. Some folks call us gypsies, and we're not always welcomed into new towns with open arms. They don't mean to be unwelcoming, I suppose, but they're suspicious of who we are and what we do."

"Then at the risk of sounding forward, who are you and exactly what do you do?"

Sadie couldn't believe the words had come out of her mouth in quite that way, but Uriah just smiled at her, amusement shimmering just beneath the surface of his mesmerizing eyes.

"We're a large, extended, and musical family. We actually are gypsies, so I don't take offense to the classification. We travel the country and stop to put on shows in towns and cities to help keep our troupe fed and comfortable. Some towns we just pass through, without performing, like Salvation. It seems to me this might not be the place for a show. You've been most kind, but some of the other folks I passed on the way in didn't seem too friendly."

"The townsfolk can be a bit wary of strangers," Sadie said, nodding. "I guess Salvation is like some of the other towns you mentioned. I hope you won't take it personally. As much as the people of Salvation like to think they're on the map, they're still close-minded in many ways."

Sadie looked toward the storefront, but didn't really seem to see what was there. She seemed to drift off, as if distancing herself from the reality of the local scene.

"Sometimes I feel a longing that goes down to the very marrow of my bones," she said, "to escape the bonds of this small town and to escape my small place in it. Every bit of my life and behavior has been virtually scripted by custom and expectation. Life in a small town will do that for you. It will keep you in the exact little niche you were born into."

Sadie started a bit, shocked to have spoken revealing words from the heart to a stranger who'd requested no such insight from her soul. What must this Uriah Smith think? Dear God, it sounded as though she was nearly begging him to steal her away from life in the claustrophobic town of Salvation. Even the name of the town seemed to mock her. Her heart was screaming, every day louder now, that HER salvation lay outside of Salvation. However, this was hardly the kind of thing to share with a one-time customer passing through town.

"Heavens, Uriah, you're like a truth serum! A few questions from you and the contents of my very soul come pouring out like water from a rainspout!"

Sadie tried to laugh and make light of what she'd just confessed, but Uriah wasn't fooled by her jocular manner. Uriah Smith knew the truth when he saw it, and Sadie Marie McNamara had shared her truth with him.

As he gazed at her, he saw her for what she truly was, although she'd given him few actual details. Sadie was on the plain side, though pretty enough. She was a responsible citizen, daughter of founding members of the town, and had never married. She channeled her drive and passion into building a successful business because it was a socially acceptable way for her to satisfy some of her needs. She was undoubtedly quite involved in civic activities as well as an active member of the town's church, and Uriah bet that Sadie had nieces and nephews and was a doting aunt as well. She'd built a good life she could be proud of, that she was respected for, but Uriah could tell she wasn't truly happy.

Staring at her, Uriah had a vision of Sadie, hair unbound and flowing free, gathering flowers barefoot in a meadow and laughing. He could see her turning to him with a joyful look in her eyes before dashing to him and covering his faces with hot kisses that would leave vivid reminders on his skin.

Shaking his head slightly as if to rid himself of a ghostly vision, Uriah wondered if he was seeing what would be or what could be. There was quite a difference. Members of his family were known to see snippets of the future, unbidden, and he didn't know if he had received one of these glimpses into the future or if he was just imagining something he'd like to see. He had met hundreds of women in his life, if not thousands. Many had caught his eye, but none had snared his heart. Sadie Marie McNamara seemed to have quickly hooked a tiny piece of herself into Uriah's heart – without even trying.

Uriah realized he'd been the cause of a pregnant pause this time and quickly recovered by winking at Sadie and chuckling. "Well of course, Sadie. Don't you know that gypsies have wild and magical ways of eliciting the truth from unsuspecting ladies? That's why the men try to hide their women away from our unscrupulous ways!" He grinned and continued. "Now that you've been duly warned about the dangers you might face in my company, I wonder if you might be so bold as to accompany me on a ride in the country tomorrow. I imagine you'll attend church in the morning, so maybe late morning or early afternoon? I could pick you up here at the store. I know it would be unseemly for a gypsy to meet you at your home!"

Sadie paused for a moment, torn between what was prudent and her heart's desire. Her parents would be appalled to think she'd go out with some strange nomad, having just met him for the first time this afternoon. However, Sadie's heart was pleading with her, *Let's go! We have to go, Sadie! This is our chance, and we're taking it!* Sadie silently assented. Life was short, and her opportunities for freedom of spirit were narrowing by the day.

"I'd be pleased and honored, Uriah. Thank you for the invitation. Shall we meet here at 11 a.m.? I'll pack a picnic lunch, if you'd like."

"That would be wonderful, Miss Sadie Marie McNamara. I'll see you then."

With that, Uriah swept out of the store with the needles and thread he'd come in for and with a date that he'd had no want or need for prior to entering Sadie's shop. As he gently closed the door to the chime of bells, it occurred to Sadie that she didn't even know what instrument he played. She envied the instrument though, no matter what it was, for the contact it would regularly have with the body of Uriah Smith.

Sadie could barely contain herself as she waited for 11 a.m. on Sunday to arrive. This week's church service had to be the longest and most tedious sermon ever, although it didn't actually run a single minute longer than any other week. Pastor Sullivan believed in the quality of the message, not quantity, so he tried to keep the entire Sunday service on a regular time schedule – from nine to ten – so the parishioners would have plenty of time to socialize afterwards before heading home for supper.

Following the services, Sadie excused herself almost immediately, telling her parents she wouldn't be joining the family for brunch at her brother Phillip's house. When asked why not, she gave a vague response that she had some things to take care of at the shop. Her family was curious, but didn't pry, and Sadie walked home quickly. Her small apartment was attached to the back of her shop, and she rushed about excitedly finishing her final preparations once she stepped inside.

By the time Uriah arrived at 11 a.m., Sadie had packed lunch, had primped, and was glowing. Uriah saw the great care she'd taken in getting ready, from her neatly arranged hair to the high shine on her shoes. He decided not to tell her of his hopes for both her hair and footwear given the vision he'd had the day before. Instead he smiled and reached for her hand, saying "You look lovely, Sadie Marie." When she put her hand in his, he drew it to his lips and laid a gentle kiss on it. Sadie would swear he'd seared her hand with that seemingly innocent kiss, but when she glanced down she saw her skin was smooth and unmarked. Perhaps the true mark lay on her heart.

As the day progressed it became clear something significant was happening between Sadie and Uriah. They kept conversation light at first as they walked to the edge of town. Sadie laughingly asked when the "ride" part of their outing would come into play, and Uriah, seeing his horse tied to the tree where he'd left it, said the ride would begin now.

"Oh, I thought we'd be riding in your wagon." Sadie eyed the large horse, and wondered how she'd possibly get up on top of it.

"Well, Miss Sadie, I'm hoping you'll trust me and go along on a bit of an adventure today. My horse, Dakota, is strong enough to carry us both. Will you give it a shot?"

Sadie didn't hesitate for a moment. She was definitely weary of the same day-to-day routine she'd been following for years, and Uriah and Dakota were a welcome variation. "I trust you, Uriah. Let's saddle up!"

Uriah laughed, grabbed her by the waist, and quickly and easily lifted the slight Sadie up onto the horse. After securing the canvas bag holding their lunch onto the back of the saddle he mounted in front of her, forcing Sadie to hold onto his waist to stay on as they moved down the road away from Salvation.

Time flew by. Uriah and Sadie talked non-stop as they rode along on Dakota's wide back, and the topics became increasingly more intimate and personal. By the time they stopped for lunch in a field of wildflowers, they felt as though they'd known each other for years. After they'd eaten, Uriah followed his instinct and leaned forward toward Sadie. He lightly touched the pins holding her hair in the bun at the back of her head, and softly said, "May I?"

Sadie nodded, entranced by the nearness of Uriah and by the warmth of his breath on her cheek. He smelled of the ripe strawberries they'd just finished eating, and his lips looked as juicy as the berries had. The intent behind his question didn't register – Uriah might've asked her if she wanted to set herself on fire, and Sadie would've absently agreed to the self-immolation.

Uriah gently removed the six pins that held up Sadie's hair and, with her golden brown hair spread about her shoulders, part of his vision from the day before was realized. Sadie could feel excitement coursing through her veins – it was nearly too much to stand, given the staid existence she'd moved through from day to day. She needed to get up and move about to relieve some of her nervous energy and decided to indulge a childhood pastime. If she drove Uriah off, so be it.

"I hope you don't think my next actions rude or unbecoming, but I used to love gathering wildflowers in the meadow beside our house – barefoot. Would you like to join me in such folly?" Sadie said, then chuckled to see Uriah stripping off his footwear a split second after the words had left her mouth. "Ah, the advantages of socializing with a wild gypsy!" Sadie said through laughter.

She followed suit, and soon they'd left their picnic spot - both barefoot - and were drifting through the lush meadow, pausing here and there to gather blooms. They kept a watchful eye, lest they step on a bee buzzing about its work, and enjoyed the long, soft grass underneath their feet. Their hands drifted together, seemingly of their own accord, and it felt as if a missing piece had finally been put into place.

Instead of taking her home, Uriah took Sadie to meet his caravan – the band of family and friends with whom he traveled and performed. They'd set up camp just outside of town. Sadie had asked Uriah about his instrument during their picnic and discovered that he played the fiddle; she was eager to hear him play. After dining with the boisterous and welcoming group, they settled around a leaping campfire that had been lit against the approaching darkness. Soon, the minstrels were giving an impromptu performance for the delighted Sadie, who couldn't keep herself from smiling and clapping. Truth be told, she could barely keep herself in her seat, and when one of Uriah's teenage nephews asked her to dance, she immediately jumped up and they danced to the laughter and cheers of the performing musicians.

Once the music had wound down, Uriah and Sadie retired to his covered wagon. The canvas cover had already been mended with the supplies Uriah had purchased in her shop the day before, and they settled into the small space, which was made cozy by lamplight and soft bedding on the floor of the wagon. They talked for hours, and when Uriah introduced the idea of Sadie sharing life with him on the road, he was honest about both the advantages and the disadvantages. The variety, excitement, and freedom were tempered by sometimes difficult physical conditions, prejudice, and a lot of time on the wagon's seat traveling from one place to another.

"I'm sure you'll think me mad for bringing this up so soon, but we're leaving town Tuesday morning, and I'd love for you to come with us. I'd like you to be my wife, Sadie Marie McNamara." Uriah's eyes radiated the depth of emotion he felt, which he was trying to convey lest she think he was insincere.

"Yes, Uriah, yes! I will join you, and I will marry you. I will gladly travel with you – we'll face whatever comes our way, together. However, I do ask one thing: Let's marry after we've left Salvation, not before. Perhaps we can find a justice of the peace in the next town to perform the service. I'm not ashamed of our extremely brief engagement, and I'm not reluctant to leave town, but I need to make a clean break -

and it will help if I can keep my explanations minimal on the front end."

Uriah understood all too well the need to leave first and to answer questions later. "Of course, Sadie. Whatever you think is best."

They talked on, planning and dreaming, until dawn was about to burst out into a new day, then finally fell asleep, stretched out next to each other, limbs intertwined. Sadie fell asleep with her head on Uriah's chest. She'd never slept better than she had in those few hours with Uriah.

On Monday, and Sadie was busy from the time Uriah delivered her to her door to the time she went to sleep in her bed - for the last time - that night. She had all sorts of life-changing tasks to see to while also trying to keep up the appearance of it being just another day in Salvation. Her first order of business was to visit the bank.

Sadie had been a frugal and prudent business owner. She owned her store, apartment, and stock outright and had saved quite a bit of money to boot. She met with Mr. Carlson, the bank manager, and said she might be doing some traveling later in the year. She wanted to verify that she could access her account and withdraw money from afar, by wire, if she needed to. Mr. Carlson assured her she could. It might take a few days, but it was possible. Sadie thanked him for the information and then approached a teller to withdraw some money for traveling necessities and spending money.

Sadie McNamara was definitely in love, but that didn't make her foolish. She was sure that Uriah was true and genuine, but she would keep her earnings and savings to herself until she was sure their relationship would last. She was completely invested in their new life together and was willing to leap. She also wanted to have some security should the unexpected happen.

Her next stop was the general store, where she purchased things she might need on the road — "woman's items" and other supplies. She avoided any in-depth conversations with the clerk, saying she had to rush back to her own store. She did need to hurry, although she mainly wanted to avoid questions about why she needed eight bars of her favorite soap when she usually purchased two at a time.

Back at her shop, Sadie decided to open the store. She really didn't want the distraction of customers, but she also didn't want to raise any red flags as she prepared for her escape. She prayed she wouldn't get any customers, then said a silent prayer of thanks that there was a lag in custom orders. The nightgown she'd finished after waiting on Uriah on Saturday had been the last item due to a customer, and she'd already had the order delivered to the Jones residence.

Sadie packed what she could, which was a quick task given that she couldn't take much with her due to limited space in Uriah's wagon. She took essential everyday wear, a few dressy ensembles, and a handful of sentimental items like a Bible, some photos, a few cherished books, and her favorite silver sewing scissors.

Next, she tidied up the shop and entered a few missing entries in her bookkeeping ledger so that everything would be in perfect order when she left. With business out of the way, Sadie prepared her gown for the next day. The wedding gown she'd made twenty years ago was a simple design, so it didn't look dated. It was made of exquisite materials, and each stitch had been perfectly executed. Sadie had originally made the gown and veil in all white. However the new sense of "bold and free" that had infused her with the audacity run away with Uriah demanded that Sadie add some color to the ensemble. Who was she to refuse?

Sadie tried the dress on before accenting it and was thrilled to find it that it still fit perfectly; she'd maintained her figure all these years. Now came the fun part. Raiding the stash of ribbons and decorative trims she had for sale, Sadie headed directly to the purples. She was most fond of a purple that was on the pinker side, versus the blue side, and decided to use a lush, velvet ribbon to trim the waist. She also added some purple beads around the neckline; they sparkled like tiny jewels. Finally, Sadie crafted a narrow wreath, which she would wear atop her flowing hair. The wreath featured more of the purple velvet ribbon in a narrower width, tiny fabric flowers in lavender, white, and purple, and deep green velvet leaves.

As the afternoon wound down, Sadie sat at her desk one last time and wrote a long letter to her family. She was somewhat daunted when she sat down, wondering how to explain something that would seem shocking and impulsive to those who knew her. Ultimately, she decided to simply lay out the facts. She'd met someone and was leaving Salvation to be with him. They'd be married immediately, and she couldn't be happier to have found him. She was sorry not to have included her family in the decision, rapid as it was, but thought it was best for everyone concerned. Her mind was made up and they'd undoubtedly have questions and caution her against haste.

Sadie also made sure to address business matters and explained she was leaving everything to them to do with as they wished. They could take over the shop and run it or sell it and all its contents – along with her attached apartment and its contents. The assets were theirs to enjoy, minus her personal accounts with the bank. She concluded the letter with a dose of reality, letting them know she was prepared for an unfavorable reaction.

I have no doubt you'll think I've gone mad for running off with a gypsy - a nomadic fiddler - and so I'll leave it up to you to explain my hasty departure to the folks of Salvation. If you're ashamed, you're welcome to say I've been committed to an asylum or that I've left to travel the world solo — what's said after I've taken my leave is of no consequence to me. I'll write from a stop along the road, to let you know I'm okay, and while I hope you'll continue to have contact with me in the future, I certainly won't expect it of you. I'm aware of the risks I'm taking with this bold change. I love you all deeply, and wish you well, and I hope you'll wish me well too.

Enclosed is the key to the shop as well as the key to my apartment.

All my love,
Sadie

After dropping the letter at the post office and requesting delivery to her parents the following day, Sadie went home and retired early. Tuesday would be a momentous day.

Uriah picked up Sadie just before dawn, as arranged, and they loaded her belongings into the covered wagon in silence, as stealthily as thieves hoping to get away with their crime scot-free. They didn't say a word, yet they were nearly shouting their love and excitement when their eyes met. Once her possessions were stowed, Sadie locked the door one final time and said a silent goodbye. She'd lived there for nearly twenty years. She was prepared for tears of nostalgia, but only felt excitement and happiness for her new life and new love.

Sadie thought they'd join the caravan immediately and was surprised when Uriah said the group would be along in a few hours. When he stopped the wagon along the side of the road, pulled by the lone, mammoth horse, Dakota, Sadie realized they'd stopped at "their meadow" – where they had picnicked two days before. He left the road and drove toward a cluster of trees. Once safely parked, Uriah lifted Sadie down from the wagon as the sun started rising in the sky. He drew her along to the center of "their" meadow, then grasped her hands in his, looking down into Sadie's upturned face.

"We won't officially marry until this afternoon when we reach Tanner, but I pledge my love to you now, Sadie Marie McNamara. I promise to love you, laugh with you, dance with you, and always be faithful to you. Although I don't have jewels to present to you as a symbol of my commitment, I hope you'll accept my heart instead."

Sadie's eyes started to glimmer upon hearing Uriah's words, and as she took a steadying breath – lest she be overcome by emotion – she glanced around them and said a reverent, "Oh Uriah!"

The meadow was filled with thousands of tiny dewdrops clinging to the grass and wildflowers that were slowly raising their faces to the sun as it climbed ever higher in the sky. The sun was also drawing out the sweet floral scent of the blooms. Sadie drank in the sight of the thousands of diamonds that she could carry in her heart forever and knew the moment was much more precious than any tangible trinket could ever be.

Uriah leaned in to kiss his newly claimed bride, then reached down and lifted Sadie into his arms. They had plenty of time before they joined the rest of the caravan later that morning - time they'd use to get to know each other even better.

While Sadie and Uriah sequestered themselves in the wagon, the rest of nature went about its business. The bees hummed, dancing from flower to flower. The birds called to each other from the trees. And Sadie learned firsthand about "the birds and the bees," finally understanding what all the fuss was about.

Second Thoughts

Melissa Brower didn't like to think of herself as materialistic or opportunistic, but she was starting to realize that might very well be the case. Why else would she have accepted Jacob's marriage proposal?

On the surface he seemed like the perfect man. He was wealthy, well educated, hardworking, gorgeous, and attentive. He showered her with lavish gifts, treated her to dinners at the most exclusive restaurants in Los Angeles, and seemed utterly devoted to her and her alone. Her friends constantly told her what a catch he was, and tried to be happy for her. Recognizing their veiled jealousy, she often attempted to downplay some of her good fortune.

For example, she didn't tell her friends about the time he'd had ten dozen long-stemmed red roses delivered to her on their ten-week anniversary. Nor did she tell them about the time they'd been shopping on Rodeo Drive and she'd broken the heel on her shoe. He'd whisked her into a nearby store and insisted she pick out a pair of Jimmy Choo's just so she'd have something to wear. Although Melissa enjoyed wearing beautiful and stylish clothes, the idea of wearing that much money on her feet was a bit unsettling.

Jacob seemed to do something incredibly sweet and over the top nearly every week, which sometimes made Melissa question whether it was too good to be true. In fact, it was. Over time, Melissa became increasingly concerned about Jacob's behavior, but she justified their continued involvement by telling herself he'd never laid a hand on her – although this didn't change the fact that Jacob had two distinct sides to his personality.

Most of the time he was the charming and attentive man of Melissa's dreams. However, from time to time, he would become cold, distant, snotty, impatient, and mean. The first time his "darker side" had reared its ugly head, Melissa had attributed it to work stress. He'd been under incredible amounts of pressure at work doing – well, Melissa wasn't exactly clear on what he did. It was investment banking or something like that. All she knew for sure was that it had been making him crabby.

She had been putting the final touches on her makeup when she heard Jacob nearly shout from the living room. "For the love of God, Melissa, hurry up! We have reservations! You're going to dinner, not competing in a fucking beauty pageant!" The contempt in his voice had chilled her blood and knotted her stomach.

Appalled by his outburst, she pasted on a smile and ignored it - never mind that he had been early and that she had been trying to hurry so he wouldn't be sitting idle. Apparently Melissa made her first deal with the devil that very day by ignoring his rancor and sliding tensely out the door to keep their reservation at The Ivy. *Screw him*, Melissa thought. *I'm not giving up my chance to see and be seen. Who knows who will be at The Ivy tonight?* It was a favored spot amongst the Hollywood set, and Melissa was going.

Her decision was easy to justify the next day when he'd apologized sorrowfully and gifted her with a sterling silver necklace from Tiffany & Co. The little blue box and his contrite expression convinced her that his actions the night before had been a fluke – an aberration – something that wouldn't be repeated.

Wishful thinking.

The pattern continued to repeat over the following months. In the beginning, Jacob's "flare-ups" were few and far between. However, over time, he became increasingly toxic – and Melissa began to wonder if the dinners, the nights at exclusive clubs, the gifts, and his often rapt attention were worth the darkness that all the more frequently enveloped him. The snide remarks, the hostility, the silent treatment, the slamming doors, and the days he didn't contact her at all began to trouble her more and more.

Just when Melissa was beginning to truly doubt the sanity of the relationship, Jacob swooped in with something she couldn't resist: a down-on-one-knee proposal and a three-carat diamond ring. The devil whispered in her ear as Jacob was proposing, reminding Melissa about all the romantic and generous things Jacob had done for her, how sweet and funny he could be, how much Jacob cared for her, and what a handsome man he was. These whisperings, along with the dazzling stone in a platinum Tiffany setting and her first honest-to-God proposal, drowned out the good sense that was bubbling to the surface and trying to force the words "Thank you, but no" from her lips.

Even in that moment, when joy and harsh reality were colliding in her mind and Jacob was sliding the engagement ring on her left ring finger, Melissa knew the deal was complete. The devil had won. The ring weighed heavily on both her hand and heart, but oh how it sparkled!

Shortly after the engagement, with her mixed emotions still roiling, Melissa met her father for lunch, where she was presented with a precious and sentimental gift: a photo of her great-grandparents on her mother's side.

"Your mother wanted you to have some of the Petrov family photos after you married, and since you're engaged I thought I'd start with this one. This is a picture of her mother's parents, taken shortly after they married."

Melissa smiled. "Thanks, Daddy, thank you so much." She looked down at the photo. "Aren't they a handsome couple?"

"They certainly are. I don't know much about them, I'm afraid. They seem to be shrouded in a bit of mystery, but

I do recall hearing that your great-grandmother died when her children were still quite young."

"Pity," Melissa murmured, distracted by both the mention of mystery and the loss she still felt for her mother. Her mom had died of cancer when Melissa was in high school, but it seemed like it was just yesterday.

Although a bit nervous about the big step she and Jacob were taking, Melissa wasn't exactly having second thoughts – not quite. Melissa knew Jacob was unpredictable and difficult, but she'd always thought that he had her best interest at heart – deep down – even if he lost control of himself from time to time. Fortunately, soon after their engagement, Jacob illustrated quite clearly that he had his best interests at heart, first and foremost. Unfortunately, he'd risked her well-being to get what he wanted.

The senior staff at Jacob's investment firm, where he was a junior executive, had invited them to a dinner party at the CEO's home. They were eager to meet Jacob's fiancée, and he was desperate to make a good impression. Friday, the day before the event, Melissa started feeling a bit run down and achy. Afraid she might be coming down with something yet knowing how important the evening was to Jacob, she prayed she'd be fine and that everything would go perfectly. However, by Saturday morning, she felt as though she'd been run over by a truck. It was undeniable: She had the flu. Her symptoms had multiplied: headache, sore throat, extreme fatigue, chills, and a high fever. Dreading his response, she called Jacob to tell him the bad news. When she explained she was sick with the flu and suggested they reschedule the dinner, he was silent for a very long moment. Melissa's heart dropped. She knew this was not going to go well at all.

"Reschedule?" Jacob raged, venom dripping from his voice. "Do you have any idea how difficult it was to schedule something like this in the first place? These men have taken time from their busy lives to welcome and meet you, and you can't get it together and show up? They're top-level executives with schedules and responsibilities that would make your pretty little head swim. They don't have time to monkey around with the likes of you. You will attend, you will medicate yourself properly to disguise your illness, and you will make me proud. I will pick you up promptly at 5:30 p.m. for our drive to Mr. Parker's home in Pacific Palisades. Be ready on time."

He left off the "or else," but it was certainly implied as the line went dead.

Stunned into compliance, partially because she was burning with fever and was borderline delirious, Melissa ran to the nearest pharmacy and bought the strongest over-the-counter medication she could find. She raced back home, took the coldest shower she could tolerate - despite the fact that she was already freezing from the chills - and got dressed. She carefully styled her thick chestnut hair and applied her makeup, then added the jewelry and clutch she'd chosen for her outfit days before getting sick. She did these things woodenly, mechanically, driven forward on automatic pilot that belied the war raging on within her body. Through it all, the three-carat diamond in her engagement ring winked wickedly at her, mocking her, reminding her that she'd brought this on herself. The devil made another appearance too, whispering in Melissa's ear that she just had to make it through one measly dinner party; she couldn't really blame Jacob for getting the tiniest bit upset, could she?

When Jacob picked her up, promptly at 5:30, he was the picture of kindness and calm. He guided her gently to his car while complimenting her on how stunning she looked. For a moment, in her weakened state, Melissa thought she must've imagined the acidic phone call from earlier in the day. Surely she imagined it, for right now he was the embodiment of a caring fiancé.

When they arrived at Tom Parker's gated mansion and Jacob helped her out of his low-slung Porsche Boxster, Melissa swayed as she stood. In that instant, a dark gleam appeared in Jacob's steel grey eyes.

"Don't you dare faint, Melissa. If you do, you'll be so very sorry," he hissed. He gripped her upper arm excruciatingly tightly as he propelled her to the front door. Melissa was convinced that his fingers would have to be surgically removed given how deep they were gouging into her skin.

The door, answered by one of the staff, opened silkily, and they were ushered inside. Her light wrap was whisked away, and they moved quickly through the foyer toward the formal living room to the left of the entry. Last to arrive, they joined three other couples in the richly appointed room, including the hosts, Tom and Denise Parker.

Melissa was absolutely burning up by this time. The fever had reached a new threshold, and her eyes were glassy. She bit the inside of her cheek to stay focused as she approached the first person with a hand held out to her. Jacob sounded as if he spoke from the bottom of a well. "Mr. Parker, this is my fiancée, Melissa Brower."

Melissa managed to grasp his hand and respond, "It's such a pleasure to meet you, Mr. Parker. Thank you so much for inviting us to your home. It's lovely."

Tom Parker was no fool. When he saw the shine to her eyes, noted the faint sheen of sweat that appeared on her brow, and felt the incredible heat radiating from Melissa's skin, he knew something was terribly awry. He also saw the hard edge in his employee's eyes and the death grip Jacob had on the young lady's arm, as if determined to move Melissa forward through sheer will despite the fact that she was clearly sick.

"My goodness, Melissa, you're just as beautiful as Jacob said – if not more so. I can't help but notice though, dear, that you're simply burning up. Are you unwell?" Tom Parker queried with genuine concern evident in his voice. He and his wife, Denise, had a daughter around Melissa's age.

Melissa just stared at him for a moment as his voice echoed faintly in her ears, trying to make her mouth work and force out the words that would assure him she was fine. They wouldn't come.

Instead, she fainted dead away in the Parkers' living room.

She remembered little of the ambulance ride to the hospital – just flashes of light and sound. There was also incredible cold as the paramedics blanketed her with ice packs in an attempt to bring down her soaring fever. Then began what she'd later call the "hallucinatory triple feature," which she remembered with utter clarity.

The first feature was a montage of sorts starring her maternal great-grandparents, Lena and Ivan Petrov. It would've been even stranger if her dad hadn't given her the family photo just a week or two before, but it was still odd to see them and in such great detail. The first "scene" was of the couple early in their courtship, followed by the handsome couple on their momentous wedding day.

Next was a breakfast, with Ivan giving Lena the silent treatment and glaring at her angrily. Then, one evening, Melissa saw Ivan yelling at Lena, throwing a heavy-cut glass tumbler at a mirror in their bedroom before storming out. Poor Lena was left sobbing and slowly went about the process of cleaning up while trying not to cut herself on the broken glass and mirror. Their young children came running, frightened by the noise, but Lena kept them shut away from the harshness of the scene. She hastily dried her tears, cracked the door, assured them everything was fine, and sent them off to play so they wouldn't worry. Once they were safely away, she went back to the mess at hand.

The final scene in this feature was the hardest to witness. Ivan was speaking to Lena angrily, voice rising to a shout. He grabbed her, shook her by the shoulders, and then slapped her viciously with his right hand. The slap itself wasn't enough to kill her, but she struck her head on the edge of the marble hearth as she fell to the ground. The latter blow was enough to kill her. Time stood still as the color drained from Ivan's face when he realized that Lena wasn't moving. He finally felt for the pulse at her neck. Feeling none, he gathered his wife in his arms and started to sob. "Please don't leave me, Lena, please! Please don't die! I didn't mean to hurt you, I swear! I don't know what came over me. I love you, Lena, please don't go!"

The second feature was Lena's funeral; Melissa herself was in attendance. She entered from the rear of the room and saw many people there to mourn her great grandmother's death. They were dressed in the funeral clothes of the time, heavy and black. Melissa was wearing the ensemble she'd chosen for the dinner party at the Parkers' home, but no one seemed to notice her or her strange apparel. An open casket, banked by huge and fragrant flower arrangements, dominated the front of the room, and Melissa was drawn to it. When she reached the casket, she looked down onto her great-grandmother's face. She looked sweet and tranquil, as if she were just napping rather than being the victim of a violent death. Melissa's heart leapt into her throat as Lena's eyes suddenly snapped open and shifted their focus to the right to look directly at Melissa before she began speaking softly.

"My dear child, do not mistake passionate behavior for love. Those who truly love you will protect you from harm, not inflict the harm. Those who truly love you will care for you, not endanger you for their personal agenda." Her eyes lingered on Melissa a moment longer, compelling brown pools of love that reinforced the words she'd just spoken, then they closed. Lena's face was again the picture of calm and stillness – and death.

The third and final feature was set in a cemetery. Melissa had been there before and quickly recognized it – even in the midst of her fever-induced hallucination. Her great-grandmother, grandmother, and mother were all buried in this cemetery. Three generations of Petrov women in the same hallowed ground. It was both incredibly sweet and very sad. Melissa approached her great-grandmother's headstone, behind which the three women were seated, drinking tea. The milk and sugar containers rested on the top of the wide headstone, and each woman had a pressed napkin on her lap and a matching cup and saucer in her hands. Melissa fought to keep herself from bawling aloud, she missed her mom so much. Her grandma too!

Her mother and grandmother looked to Lena to speak first, who demurred, saying, "I've already said my piece."

Her grandma was next. "Honey, you've gotten in over your head. Jacob may mean well, but we're not convinced that he does. Regardless, he doesn't treat you well. We can't abide it, and neither should you." Her grandmother was loving, but firm.

Finally, her mother spoke. "My precious Melissa, you've grown up to be such a lovely young woman. Don't let the beauty and the good inside you be smothered by the dark spirit of another. Don't let the flame of your life and spirit be extinguished needlessly by anyone – no matter how much they claim to love you." Her mother's words were like the gentle caresses she'd received as a small child with her head on her mom's lap, hair smoothed back from her forehead in a soothing rhythm. They were comfort, safety.

Looking at all three women, tears streaming from her eyes, Melissa managed to choke out "You're all right." Sobbing, she added, "I love you all so much. Can I stay here with you? Mom, Grandma – I've missed you so much, and would love to get to know Great-grandma Lena. I have so many things I want to ask all of you and so much to learn. I've felt so empty without you in my life, and I clearly need your guidance!"

It was too late though; the three Petrov women were already fading from sight. As the final feature faded to black, Melissa could feel their love and strength embracing her, preparing her for the next part of her journey.

Melissa woke the next morning in a private hospital room. Her dad was dozing in a chair in the corner, his rumpled clothes indicating an uncomfortable overnight stay in that very chair. Jacob was nowhere to be seen, although they'd been together at the Parkers' home the last time she'd been fully conscious. Her engagement ring was in its usual place, glinting provocatively at her in the morning light. Melissa slipped it off her finger with solemn resolve.

Just then her dad woke up, yawning and stretching. He jumped up when he saw she was awake and gave her a gentle hug and kiss. He explained that he'd been summoned to the hospital last night. The doctors were desperate to break her fever while he'd stood vigil, waiting for his only child to win the fight against her illness. It was nearly 2 a.m. before the tide had turned and her body had started to cool, but he still wouldn't leave her side. It was the common flu, he explained, but the severity of the fever had put Melissa in extreme danger.

"Was Jacob here, too?" Melissa asked, morbidly curious.

"Well, briefly. When the doctors explained it might be some time before there was a change in your condition, he said he was going home – to call him if I needed something. He said it seemed there was nothing he could do, so why lose sleep?" The tension in her dad's jaw as he spoke indicated how he felt about both Jacob and his course of action, although he was trying desperately to sound neutral.

"Oh." Melissa gestured to him to raise the head of her hospital bed so she was nearly sitting upright.

Just then Jacob rushed in, the picture of concern. He carried a lush bouquet of lilies, Melissa's favorite flowers, and immediately drew to her right side, where he placed the flowers on the side table and reached for her hand. He stopped mid-reach when he saw the engagement ring wasn't in its place on her other hand.

"Babe, are you feeling better? That was quite a scare you gave us last night, right Mr. Brower?" Melissa's father remained silent, and Jacob looked at Melissa for reassurance.

"I'm sorry to have worried you. You seem well rested though, which is a blessing." Melissa kept her voice light, although she was clearly voicing a little post-fever sarcasm.

"Yes, well, I wanted to make sure I was in good shape so I could help take care of you today. I brought you some lilies, Melissa. I know how much you like them." His curiosity finally got the better of him. "Did the hospital staff stow your engagement ring for safekeeping?"

Melissa held out her right hand, palm up, offering him the ring. "No, Jacob. I took it off so I could return it to you – for good. I'm calling off our engagement."

Jacob's eyes nearly shot out of his skull when he saw the ring and took in the words she'd said. "Honey, I know you're sick and that last night didn't turn out quite as we'd planned, but you can't mean this. You know how much I love you!"

"I do mean it."

"Mr. Brower, can we please have a moment alone? I'd really like to talk to Melissa in private." Jacob was getting angry, but was working double time to conceal it.

"There's no need to leave, Dad. I'd prefer that you stay, actually. I'm sorry Jacob; I just don't think we're compatible. However, I wish you all the best." Melissa still held the ring out to Jacob.

Seeing that her resolve was unwavering, he finally took the ring. He fingered it for a moment, glancing darkly from Melissa to her father, displeasure pulsing through his veins.

Mr. Brower finally spoke up. "Although we've only met on a few brief occasions, I feel as though I know so much about you, Jacob. Melissa told me exactly where you live, where you work – everything. Should anything odd come up, anything that might need resolving, I know precisely where to find you." It wasn't an overt threat, just a thinly veiled one – an assertion of protection for his daughter.

Following a terse "Fine, Melissa – goodbye!" Jacob spun on his heel and strode out of the room, the siren song of the three-carat diamond ring smothered in his fiercely clenched fist.

Melissa breathed a deep sigh of relief and felt a heavy weight lift from her body, heart, and spirit. She looked up at the man standing to her left. "Thanks, Dad."

Bending down, her dad gently smoothed her hair back from her forehead, like she was a child again, and kissed her just below her hairline. "You're welcome, sweetie. It must've been a difficult decision to make, but I'm sure you made the right choice." Straightening, he smiled and looked down at his pensive daughter.

"In the end, it wasn't so hard after all. This is going to sound strange, but while I was unconscious I was guided to my decision by three angels who were drinking tea together in the cemetery." Melissa smiled, raised the head of the bed a tiny bit more with the controls to her left, and began to tell her dad all about her "hallucinatory triple feature." She knew he'd understand.

Cast from a Different Mold

Elsa and Peter McKenzie were two of the oddest children alive. Their parents hated to admit it, but it was true. When Elsa was born, they had such hopes for their fair-haired daughter and expected to love their first-born unconditionally and immediately. They thought she was beautiful and precious, of course, but they didn't really warm to her. Actually, they finally admitted that Elsa didn't warm to them.

She always seemed detached, even as an infant. It was as if she was observing each moment instead of being a part of it; this trend continued as she grew into a toddler and then became a small child. She rarely laughed or smiled. She would go through the motions of hugging and kissing her parents, stiffly, but she didn't seem to exchange or feel any warmth. Elsa didn't speak to them much either, although she understood them perfectly and spoke clearly and effectively when she chose to.

At first Mr. and Mrs. McKenzie didn't discuss such peculiarities with each other. They each pretended everything was normal, as if theirs was a happy family life instead of a stilted one. Neither wanted to be the first to mention their daughter's "quirks", so they focused on the positive.

"She has your beautiful, flaxen hair, Robert. What a lucky little girl," Tess McKenzie said, trying to look on the bright side. "I'd give my right arm for hair like that, instead of this unruly red mass."

Robert McKenzie, not to be outdone by his wife, countered with, "Ah, but she's got your lovely peaches-and-cream complexion, Tess." Better to share such banalities than address the fact that their child was wooden and distant.

They were long overdue for an honest discussion when they finally threw up their hands – together – and brought it out into the open. They started small, mentioning that perhaps Elsa wasn't as socially interactive as she might be. They moved on to address the fact that she wasn't warm to them or anyone else, and with her piercing eyes she could be downright spooky. They concluded with the realization that if she didn't break out of her icy shell, she would likely become an old maid, living at home with them for the rest of their lives. The idea genuinely scared the wits out of them. They decided they'd have to try something - anything - to get their daughter on a more conventional behavioral path.

First they tried taking her to Doctor Gumble, who examined Elsa, but couldn't find anything wrong with her. He suggested that perhaps she just needed some more play time with children her own age. Robert and Tess arranged for Elsa to play regularly with neighbor children and with her cousins, but nothing changed. Their little girl would just sit and watch, not joining in the play, so the McKenzies had to try something else to get through to Elsa.

When Tess became pregnant with their second child, both husband and wife were thrilled. They were certain a baby was just the thing they needed to bring Elsa out of her stupor and help her relate to the things and people around her better. They didn't count on their second child behaving just the same as Elsa.

Peter was born on a Tuesday morning and was the spitting image of his older sister: the same gorgeous skin, the same light hair, and the same eyes. As time passed, it became clear that their son was "removed" as well, and the McKenzies were crushed. They made a concerted effort with each child every day while never letting on that they were uncomfortable with their offspring. In reality, they were at their wit's end. And genuinely alarmed, if truth be told.

Tess and Robert tried to analyze what made the children look particularly odd, aside from their stillness and their behavior, and decided their eyes were particularly disconcerting. Elsa's and Peter's eyes were quite changeable, although Robert and Tess weren't able to identify what brought about the variation in their eye color. Their eyes were often the color of blue glacial ice, with about as much warmth emanating from them. The areas around their pupils appeared to be flecked with black, as if the rock crushed to create a glacier's moraine had been ground and dragged into their eyes. Sometimes their eyes were darker, more of a deep blue-green. It was then that they silently seemed to be peeking into others' very souls, and the elder McKenzies made sure to keep smiles on their faces, lest their children clue into their unease.

The incident that gave Tess and Robert the most pause — and nearly stopped Robert's heart — occurred the night of a big storm. The rain started at bedtime and had been tapping the roof insistently for hours when the thunder and lightning began. Robert lay on his right side, facing away from the window; he opened his eyes after the first big roll of thunder. When the lightning flashed brilliantly, illuminating the room through the sheer curtains at the window, Robert saw Elsa standing about two feet away from him, staring directly at him and inexplicably holding a silver buttonhook in her left hand, the metal glinting at her shoulder level. Robert's mouth went dry at the sight and he nearly pissed himself.

Trying desperately to appear calm, Robert said, "What are you doing up, Elsa? Did the storm wake you?"

Elsa didn't answer, just continued to stare, buttonhook in hand.

"Why are you holding Mother's buttonhook, sweetheart?" Robert asked, almost afraid she'd answer him this time - either with a frank and horrifying answer or with a swift jab-and-twist to the eye. Elsa didn't seem to realize she had the buttonhook in her hand, which was nearly as disturbing as the possibilities already rolling around Robert's head. She turned her head slightly to the left, saw it, and wordlessly lowered her hand. Then she silently turned and walked out of the room. The next spotlight blast of lightning shone on the empty space where Elsa had been standing. Robert wished the moment had been a bad dream, but he knew that what he'd seen had really happened. In that moment he made a silent vow to himself and his wife, who was sleeping and was still blissfully unaware of what had occurred: He and Tess would be locking their bedroom door at night from then on. He knew Tess would agree once he filled her in on the buttonhook incident in the morning.

Tess and Robert discussed the situation the next day, locked in their room and whispering, lest their bewildering children hear them, take offense, and come after them with knitting needles, the ice pick, or some other sharp metal implement. They acknowledged their reluctance to have more children, in case subsequent offspring were like their first two, in which case they'd be outnumbered. They wracked their brains, trying to figure out how to help their children – and themselves – but no light shone down from the heavens to illuminate the answer.

In the meantime, each day was an eerie eternity with Elsa and Peter. Unable to imagine three sets of chilling eyes looking up at him, Robert sought out and used products reputed to prevent pregnancy. He and Tess tried condoms made of both latex and the more traditional sheath made from sheep's intestines. They were never sure which type failed them, they only knew that, when Tess' abdomen began to swell yet again, the alarm they were already feeling grew into a constant state of apprehension with a sprinkling of terror that sparkled on the surface of their lives like poison-laced sugar. Tess, who had been a happy and glowing mother-to-be during her first two pregnancies, looked pale and nervous most of the time during her third, as if she had just seen a ghost – or expected to see one lurking around the next corner.

Robert was trying to appear calm for Tess' sake, but he was having a hard time as well. He hid a small hunting knife in the top drawer of his bedside table, although he could never explain to himself why he did it – or exactly what he hoped to prevent by having it there. He certainly didn't tell Tess about having a knife within arm's reach of their bed. He didn't want to worry her, given that she already seemed to be carrying the weight of the world in her womb. When his mind would skitter to the knife in the drawer and why he felt a need for it, he'd toss the thought away quickly, as if it was a smooth, oval-shaped stone he was skipping across a pond, *splosh-splosh-splosh-splosh-splosh*, before it sank and disappeared.

The birth of their third child was an unpleasant ordeal. When her contractions began, Tess whispered to her husband. "Robert, please stay with me. I'm so frightened." Her eyes filled with tears, and he knew he had to stay and "welcome" their new baby with her even though it was custom for only womenfolk and the doctor to occupy the birthing room.

Tess' labor dragged on for hours, as if her body was unwilling to release the unborn baby into the world as it knew the child would only bring pain and heartache. Finally spent, Tess could no longer fight the contractions and fell into a reluctant, troubled sleep, at which point the child made its slippery and silent arrival into the world.

Doctor Gumble said, "Congratulations, Robert, you and Tess have another baby girl!"

Robert thanked the doctor politely despite his certainty that congratulations weren't actually in order. Holding his wife's hand in his, Robert leaned down and whispered in her ear. "It'll be okay, Tess. It'll be okay." Tess' brow furrowed as she dozed fitfully, and Robert wasn't sure whether she'd heard him or not.

When Tess and Robert introduced Peter and Elsa to their new baby sister, Charlotte, the two older children seemed quite interested in the new baby. They didn't say a word to their parents or each other, but looked intently at the infant. They seemed particularly fascinated when Charlotte awoke and opened her eyes. At first her eyes appeared glacier blue, but after a minute of looking at Peter and Elsa they settled into a deep blue-green. Tess and Robert glanced at each other over the children's heads and compared notes later - after the older children were in bed and baby Charlotte was sleeping in her bassinet. They agreed that Elsa, Peter, and infant Charlotte had appeared to be talking to each other silently, with their eyes.

Months passed without further incident, and the elder McKenzies began to relax just the tiniest bit. They still locked their bedroom door at night. They still tried to foster warm relationships with their three children. They were still met with few words and long stares that left them feeling as though an icy finger was running down their spines. However, it had become commonplace. They were uncomfortable in their home every day and were a bit fearful every night, but they knew they had to move forward and continue to care for their children.

One spring day Doctor Gumble stopped by the McKenzie home to perform a checkup on Charlotte, who had just celebrated her first birthday. Both Robert and Tess wanted to be home for the checkup, so Tess had set the appointment for a Saturday afternoon.

Always punctual, unless a medical emergency detained him, Doctor Gumble knocked on the McKenzies' door at two o'clock. When there was no answer, he knocked again. The door remained shut, the utter silence deafening him. Worried that something might be wrong inside, Doctor

Gumble turned the door handle and pushed the door in while calling out loudly, "Robert, Tess - are you here?"

Unprepared for the sight that met his eyes, Doctor Gumble came to an abrupt stop just inside the door. His fingers went lax, and his handsome leather and brass doctor's bag thudded sickly on the floor next to his left foot. Tess and Robert McKenzie were home, and so were their children. Tess and Robert lay at the foot of the staircase, about ten feet in front of the door. Elsa, Peter, and Charlotte stood in a semi-circle around them, with their backs to the staircase. Doctor Gumble's heart rate accelerated as his shrewd eyes took in the unnatural angles of Tess' and Robert's bodies, their still chests and slack jaws, and the looks that passed between the three McKenzie children. Even young Charlotte looked smug as the three of them stared down at their fallen parents.

Fighting the urge to run, Doctor Gumble asked in as steady a voice as he could muster, "What happened to your parents, children?"

Elsa, the eldest, answered for all three of them, speaking in a frostbitten monotone. "They tripped and fell down the staircase." She raised her eyes to the doctor's eyes, and he saw that they seemed to change from light blue to deep blue-green in an instant. Terrified, and afraid for his own life, Doctor Gumble couldn't help but wonder if she really was reading his thoughts, as she seemed to be, or if he was simply going mad.

The Language of Flowers

Laurel had never believed in love at first sight, but a chance encounter changed her mind. Early one Saturday morning she headed out of her Manhattan studio apartment, grabbing coffee and a croissant at the corner coffee shop before heading to the Annex Antique Fair and Flea Market on 6th Avenue. It was a misty morning, and the sun was just rising, peeking through the veil of moisture in the air. The instant she laid eyes on him - well, actually on his picture propped up on a table in one of the antiques booths she was passing by - she knew their lives would be forever intertwined. Enthralled, she stopped, picked up the photo, and felt the magic wash over her.

The man in the vintage photo wasn't the most handsome man she'd ever seen, but there was definitely something special about him. He was attractive, and he looked kind and attentive, as if he noticed people and things, even if they were seemingly unremarkable. Such a quality was quite important to Laurel. She was average looking, on the slight and scrawny side. She had mousy, thin dirty blonde hair that limply hung straight down past her shoulders. Her eyes were a dull gray that were hidden behind thick glasses. She was unremarkable in virtually every way, except perhaps for how well she blended into a crowd.

Looking at the photo, Laurel just knew that he would notice her, see her for her subtle qualities. He would see past her shy exterior and look into her heart. Right there, amidst the bustle of the Antique Fair and Flea Market, Laurel Kendrick started to fall in love.

After purchasing the vintage black-and-white photo for a mere four dollars, Laurel walked briskly down the street and caught the subway home. She inspected the photo during her subway ride. There was no notation of the man's name, so she decided his name was Oliver. She continued her daydream as she made the rest of journey home and created a bit more of his history – or perhaps it was simply revealed to her.

Oliver was an artist who traveled the world capturing gorgeous landscapes on canvas. He was a kind, charming, and considerate man who wanted a wife and family. He hadn't had the chance to settle down, given that he'd been traveling and painting so many commissioned works, but Laurel knew he was just waiting for the right time and the right woman.

Back at her apartment, Laurel gave his photo a place of honor on a bookshelf and went about the rest of her day. Yet she found herself returning to the shelf every so often to gaze at Oliver's face.

Laurel met Oliver in her dreams for the first time that night. He said he was so pleased to meet her, and they spent some time getting to know each other. He didn't think it odd that a woman from the "future" had met him in their dreams. They didn't actually speak of the distance or of the years between them. It seemed it was a non-issue.

Oliver, being the Victorian-era gentleman that he was, was well acquainted with the language of flowers and the concept that each type of flower means a different thing. Presenting a particular blossom meant passing along a particular message to recipient. That night, as they were parting, Oliver said, "I hope to see you again very soon, Laurel. I truly enjoyed our time together." He'd handed her a stem of bird of paradise as he spoke.

When Laurel woke, she did a quick search on the Internet and discovered that bird of paradise translated to "strange and wonderful" in the language of flowers. Laurel turned and looked at the photo of Oliver, still propped up on the bookshelf, and knew she'd happened upon something strange and wonderful indeed.

Their relationship progressed rapidly. Laurel was essentially alone in the world, with no friends or family to distract her from the budding romance, and she became increasingly consumed with Oliver. Soon she was dreaming of him – with him – every night, and eventually she dreamt of him anytime she fell asleep, even if it was a mid-day nap.

Their "dates" were always quite chaste and proper. Oliver didn't want to take advantage of her; after all, he was a gentleman. There was no denying their attraction, although they never spoke of it. They did talk about virtually everything else though. Given that Oliver was an artist and Laurel had been an art history major in college, they had quite a lot to discuss, including the art that had come into existence since Oliver's time period, near the turn of the 20th century. Laurel took him to the Metropolitan Museum of Art at the edge of Central Park, and they spent hours looking at the creations housed in the enormous museum. Oliver was particularly interested in the work of Pablo Picasso and Jackson Pollack, and he was eager to try these new styles of painting himself, as most of the work he'd done was focused on recreating something exactly as he'd seen it in nature.

During these hours together Laurel also opened up to Oliver about her solemn and solitary life. An only child, her mother had died when she was nine; her father had died shortly before she was born. Without any extended family to care for her, Laurel had been shuttled from one foster home to another until she'd graduated from high school. A bright and painfully shy girl, she'd retreated into her studies and was the valedictorian of her high school class. She was also friendless and exceedingly plain, so her scholastic achievements were all she had to cling to.

She'd earned multiple scholarships, and hoped things would change for her in college – that she'd finally make friends and go on her first date. However, Laurel couldn't seem to find anything in common with the girls in her dormitory or classes and continued to be invisible to the males she encountered. Her years at NYU were a study in isolation, as she ate by herself and studied amidst the hushed whispers and heavy silence at the university's library.

After graduation she went to work as an art restorationist and, although her co-workers were polite, she was still held at arm's length. It made Laurel sad and a bit humiliated to admit all this to Oliver, as evidenced by the tears that spilled down her pale cheeks as she spoke, but she knew he understood when he smiled tenderly and gently wiped away her tears with the freshly laundered handkerchief he'd pulled from his breast pocket. Without saying a word he gently placed her arm through his and they walked on through museum – parading past the post-impressionist paintings lining the walls.

After one of these visits to the museum, they shared a picnic lunch in the park, where Oliver presented Laurel with a red tulip. He extended the bloom with a tender smile, and Laurel was eager to know what the flower meant. She was delighted to discover that it meant "declared love" in the language of flowers. Laurel guessed that Oliver was ready to take their relationship to another level and couldn't wait to see him again in her next dream.

Laurel lost virtually all interest in the waking world and was only interested in sleeping, where she could spend time with Oliver in the special place between their two worlds. If she wasn't working or doing other essential things like cleaning, showering, or grocery shopping, she was sleeping.

Laurel and Oliver seemed to have the magic ability to move between his time and hers, so they visited in the past and the present, enjoying their time together immensely. It was only natural that they became engaged. Laurel knew Oliver was ready for a life together the night he offered her a bouquet of violets, which meant "advancement in life" in the language of flowers. He was proposing!

They decided they'd be married in May, when the roses were in full bloom at the Brooklyn Botanic Garden. Laurel had been there many times in the past and had enviously watched bridal parties wrapped in happiness as they celebrated the joining of two lives. Laurel, who'd never even been kissed, had stared at the luminescent brides, wondering why they'd been chosen and she hadn't. Now herself engaged, she was supremely happy, knowing she was a "chosen one" too.

Laurel found the perfect engagement ring at the same antique mart where she'd "met" Oliver. It was a platinum setting featuring a small diamond that was flanked by two tiny sapphires. Sapphires were her birthstone, and Oliver agreed it was the perfect choice when he saw her wearing it that night. It was a perfect fit too, so Laurel didn't have to worry about getting the ring sized. It was clearly meant to be.

Her next wedding-related purchase was a vintage wedding dress she found at an antique store in the heart of the city. She believed that the dress had been made in the early 1900s based on the style; it too fit like a dream. The once-glorious garment needed some restoration to make it shine for the big day, and Laurel spent a weekend mending small tears, carefully hand washing it, and tacking decorative trim back on.

The last major component of wedding attire that Laurel needed for the big day was her bouquet. She conferred with Oliver to make sure the bouquet would express what they felt in their hearts and what they hoped for in their marriage. In the end she ordered a free-form bouquet with a number of different organic elements to it: full, open pink roses for perfect happiness, honeysuckle for the bonds of love, stephanotis for happiness in marriage, rosemary for remembrance, orchids for ecstasy, and poppies for dreams and eternal sleep.

Laurel had been preparing for her wedding day for more than a month by the time the momentous day arrived. She woke early and readied the apartment for their wedding night. She and Oliver had decided they'd live in the present, so they'd return to her small but well-appointed apartment later that day – after the ceremony and a celebratory meal at Laurel's favorite French restaurant, Les Sans Culottes. Laurel had already cleaned the apartment until it shined. She filled the apartment with beautiful pink roses and intoxicatingly fragrant tuberoses. She'd also brought in dozens of candles and placed them about in small clusters, hoping to make the room seem even more enticing.

Finally, Laurel prepared herself, bathing and dressing carefully. Although she didn't usually wear makeup, she applied some blush, a layer of mascara, and some rose-tinted lip-gloss. She carefully put on her dress, arranged the veil she'd found to go with it, and placed her engagement ring on her right ring finger in anticipation of receiving a wedding band on her left ring finger.

Laurel lit the dozens of candles scattered around and eyed the effects approvingly. She knew Oliver would appreciate the efforts she'd made to make their wedding day special. She could hardly wait to see him in his wedding suit, which would be graced with a stephanotis boutonnière. Laurel tenderly picked up the beautiful bouquet the florist had delivered to her that morning before going to lie down on top of the perfectly made bed. She set the photo of Oliver, her loving and kind artist, next to her on the bed, propped up against the adjacent empty pillow, and smiled adoringly at him before settling into sleep. The bouquet was held in her hands in front of her, against her abdomen, as if she were posing for a wedding portrait. A demure smile graced her lips.

As she drifted into sleep, Laurel saw herself hailing a cab downstairs in the front of her building. She asked the driver to take her to the Brooklyn Botanic Garden. Before she knew it, they'd arrived. She made her way inside, where she met Oliver and the Justice of the Peace at the agreed upon place: the Cranford Rose Garden. Home to tens of thousands of blooming roses in over 1200 varieties, the bridal couple was intoxicated by both the rich scent and the sparkling dewdrops that clustered on the flowers like gems.

The ceremony passed quickly, with both Oliver and Laurel fervently speaking words of love and devotion. They exchanged simple platinum bands that belied the complexity of their love and situation. As they neared the end of the ceremony, Laurel's already-quickened heart rate sped up even more. She'd been waiting months to kiss her true love for the first time, and the moment was nearly upon them. As they gazed into each other's eyes, Laurel and Oliver heard the Justice of the Peace say, "I now pronounce you husband and wife. Oliver, you may kiss the bride." They drifted together slowly, and the kiss they shared forged their lives together. Laurel felt a bittersweet pain fill her to the core, as if the intensity of Oliver's kiss was nearly enough to stop her heart.

As it turned out, it was precisely enough to stop her heart.

Laurel's body wasn't found until the Tuesday after their Saturday wedding. Her co-workers became concerned when she skipped work for a second consecutive day without calling in sick and sent the police to her apartment to make sure she was okay.

Two police officers were dispatched to investigate. When Laurel didn't answer the building's intercom or a knock at her door, officers Taylor and Gordon enlisted the help of the building's superintendent, who used his master key to let them in. The officers entered, quickly swept the small, tidy apartment, and found Laurel on her bed. She was utterly still and the smell of her wilting bridal bouquet mixed with the scent of her decaying body. The sight of Laurel transfixed the officers momentarily, and the superintendent wandered in behind them before they could ban him from the apartment – now a potential crime scene.

"Jesus, Mary, and Joseph!" the super exclaimed, taking in the dozens of gutted candles that had burned themselves out in crystal votive holders. "She coulda burned the whole freaking building down!"

Officers Taylor and Gordon quickly removed him from the scene and radioed the death into headquarters. It appeared to be death by natural causes as they found no signs of foul play or even overt signs of suicide, but they couldn't be sure without further investigation, an autopsy, and a toxicology report. Was this just another odd New York City death? The elaborate setup with the dress, bouquet, photo, and candles had them wondering if there wasn't more to Laurel Kendrick's demise. In the end, the only physical evidence they couldn't explain was the mark on Laurel's left ring finger: a raised, circular welt, as if she'd been burned or branded. The burn was the size and shape of a narrow wedding band.

An Inherited Trait

"For the love of God. What the hell is this?!" Debbie stared down at the contents of the package she'd just pulled from the freezer and had to face the facts. Mother was not well, not well at all. Debbie had suspected she was troubled; now she had irrefutable confirmation, proof that Mother's mental and emotional health was in jeopardy. After all, what healthy person would wrap fabric in brown butcher paper, label the package "pork roast," and stow it neatly in the freezer?

This wasn't a case of being distracted or forgetful, nor could it be chalked up to a more serious case of dementia. Mother was a fabric-collecting fiend, a hoarder, and she was trying to avoid conflict with Debbie, her only child. Debbie had recently expressed concern over her extreme case of quilting-supply-shopping fever. Debbie had "strongly suggested" that her mother not bring any more fabric into the house until she'd used some of her current stash, as their shared home was nearly bursting with the stuff already. Apparently mother was not ready to give up her vice and had resorted to creative ways of hiding her purchases instead.

Mother specialized in the acquisition of fabric – whether it was full yards, fat quarters, or something in between. However, she also gathered copious amounts of thread, batting, and the patterns to actually make the quilts. Mother had a top-of-the-line Bernina sewing machine and all the other tools she needed to produce quilts; however, production had completely dropped off.

For years mother had been a quilt-making phenomenon, creating stunning works that were given as gifts, raffled at charity events, and even hung as wall décor instead of being used as a bedcover. Mother had also won a few quilting competitions, which feathered her cap nicely. It was her "thing," and she'd taken such pleasure creating works of art that were functional as well.

All that had changed when her husband, Debbie's father, had died.

Debbie still felt a wrench in her heart every time she thought of her father, so she could only imagine how her mother felt. High school sweethearts, her parents had been married for nearly fifty years when her father had died of a massive heart attack. There was no warning, just sudden loss.

Naturally her mother had needed time to adjust, time to work through her grief. Debbie hadn't expected her to run back into her sewing room and whip up something in all black that they could use to picnic at her father's grave. However, she had assumed that her mother would eventually return to making quilts or, if she didn't have the heart for the work anymore, that she'd at least stop shopping for the quilting projects she wasn't starting or completing. Not so.

Soon a well-stocked sewing room had escaped the confines of one room and was taking over the far reaches of the house. Debbie knew this all too well because she'd moved in after her dad had died. If she hadn't taken over the third bedroom and closet, that room would've undoubtedly been filled too. What initially seemed like a good idea – namely, sharing expenses and keeping each other company - soon became slightly tense as mother became a bit reclusive and started stuffing newly acquired fabric into every empty nook and cranny. Her only social outlet these days seemed to be shopping, and Debbie knew something had to be done – the fabric stowed in the freezer just couldn't be ignored.

She stared down at the cotton fabric lying on the brown freezer paper. It was printed with a hollyhock pattern, and Debbie was certain her mother had been missing her husband when she bought it. Her parents had taken a picture in front of hollyhocks on their wedding day. Debbie knew the photo so well that it was etched in her mind. However, Debbie also knew that not every piece of fabric her mother was squirreling away was so sentimental.

Her thoughts were interrupted by a knock at the door, and she strode over to answer it. "Hi Aunt Ruby, how are you? Please come in." Debbie opened the door all the way and gestured the elderly woman inside with a wave of her hand and a smile. Debbie guided her to the living room. After offering Ruby something to drink and serving her some iced tea, they settled in comfortably to chat.

"I came by to see your mother. She cancelled our lunch plans last week, and I just wanted to come by in person and make sure she was doing okay." Ruby, her mother's aunt and Debbie's great aunt, was a vital woman. Although she was nearly eighty, she was fit and energetic.

Debbie's green eyes shone with the first glint of gathering tears as she confessed to her great aunt that she wasn't sure mother was doing well at all. "Do you have any idea what I found in the freezer just now - what she was trying to hide from me? Fabric!"

Debbie explained how her mother's once normal shopping habits had spiraled out of control and that she'd become noticeably less social. "It's almost as if she's shutting herself away from the world, while also trying to fill an internal void – with textiles! And don't even get me started on her obsession with arranging it all. She's constantly re-organizing her 'inventory,' grouping things by color or pattern or some other criteria that only she only understands. I was concerned before, Aunt Ruby, but this freezer thing takes it all to a whole new level, and I'm truly worried."

Aunt Ruby looked at Debbie and nodded to show she was listening and understood. She remained silent a minute more before asking, "Did I ever tell you about John Buckley?"

Debbie silently shook her head.

"Well, as you know I'm the family historian, and John Buckley is one of our deceased relatives – your mother's great-great grandfather to be exact. From what I've heard, he was always a bit eccentric, but he was definitely 'off' after the war. The trauma seemed to have made him worse. He was a hoarder too, you see."

Ruby paused to take a sip of her iced tea.

"John was drafted into the Civil War by the North in 1863 and, not surprisingly, his stint in the army wasn't pleasant. Not only did the men face death in battle, but they also faced rampant disease and hunger. Their rations were lousy at best, mostly consisting of salted beef or pork and hardtack – a flour biscuit. When those dismal rations were cut off, things became even bleaker for the soldiers."

Debbie's eyes were wide. "It got worse? I can't even imagine what bleaker would entail!"

"Once John's unit was cut off from supplies for nine days, and they became so hungry that it even hurt to drink water – the cramping in their guts was so bad. That experience resulted in John being truly obsessed with food when he returned home to Illinois. When he got back, he was so thin that a stiff wind could've blown him over, but he ate so much that he'd soon regained some weight. It's almost as if he was making up for all the good things he could've eaten while in the army. However, it was soon clear that he didn't just feel a physical hunger, but that it was a psychological hunger, too.

"Your great-great-great grandmother kept a full pantry - and was quite capable of keeping it properly stocked - but John started keeping his own pantry after his return. He built a small walk-in closet near the kitchen and fitted it out with rows of wooden shelves. Then he packed it to bursting with his special supplies. That poor man compulsively inventoried the contents of his pantry daily, counting the totals for each item and logging them in a ledger dedicated solely to the panty. It didn't matter that the quantities usually stayed the same or that he was the only one with a key to the pantry, he still logged the inventory totals every day.

"Occasionally there would be a small shift in the quantity of an item, for he also kept careful track of how long a particular item had been in the pantry and made sure to rotate the item in question out into the 'general pantry' for use before it spoiled. Out with one, back in with another of the same – often the next day. He got a particular sense of satisfaction when he made the last hash mark that brought the item's number back up to the magic number – nine. He had to have nine of all the items he stocked in that pantry. Nine jars of strawberry preserves. Nine sacks of flour. Nine tins of canned fish. Nine jugs of water. Nine bottles of whiskey. I imagine the number nine stuck in his head because that's how many days he went without food and supplies during the war, but that's just speculation.

"Naturally, all this drove his wife nuts – the obsessive hoarding and daily inventories, the separate and locked pantry, the key he carried with him at all times. It was a silver key, and apparently he even slept with it within arm's reach. All of this meticulous and obsessive behavior was even more frustrating for John's wife, Marie, because while he was regimented and orderly in his pantry, he was sloppy and scattered elsewhere. He might have crumbs in his beard or be wearing two different shoes, but his jars of preserves and vegetables were in a gleaming and orderly row! She wrote about all his oddities in a journal to keep from going round the bend herself, which is how I know so much about these particular Buckleys."

Ruby cleared her throat, then took another sip of tea.

"Marie noticed that John had more nightmares and became even more anxious after attending Grand Army of the Republic meetings, a veteran's organization for Union soldiers. She suspected that these reminders of his time in the army were more harmful than helpful – like scraping at a wound just when it'd begun to scab over. Eventually, at her request, she and John moved to Wisconsin, to distance themselves from the meetings and the home they'd lived in before and after John had served. Marie was hoping they'd form new, happier associations. She never told John her real reason for wanting to move, instead saying that she wanted to be near their daughter and grandchildren."

"Did it work? Did John improve in Wisconsin?" Debbie asked, curious about the outcome of this long-ago story.

"It's hard to say. Marie didn't continue writing in the journal after the move, which could be attributed to a number of things. Maybe he improved and she didn't need the release of writing, or perhaps the journal was packed away so well she didn't find it again when they arrived in Wisconsin. Unfortunately, I don't know for sure."

Debbie seemed to deflate and sank a bit deeper into the cushions of the sofa. An astute woman, she was fairly sure she knew why her great Aunt Ruby had shared this story. "So you think John had post traumatic stress disorder and maybe my mother does too?"

"I think it's quite likely. Members of the Buckley family have the tendency to be obsessive packrats on a good day. When you throw in a major trauma, like war or the sudden death of a loved one, things can get even messier."

Debbie sat quietly for a moment, pensive, then turned to the older woman seated to her right. "Thank you for sharing this information with me, Aunt Ruby. Your timing was impeccable. I was approaching my wit's end! And while I still have no idea what to do, at least I've got some context and insight. Thanks also for listening and allowing me to vent."

Ruby smiled at her great-niece and reached out to squeeze Debbie's hand. "Well, why don't we work as a team on this? Maybe we can talk with your mom and suggest some things that might break this cycle. A widow's support group could be helpful, along with some volunteer work to get her out of the house? I have a feeling we'll be able to bring her around. I'll bet there will be room for actual food in your freezer again soon, and you won't have to move all the way to Wisconsin to see a noticeable change in your mother!"

Just then Debbie's mother, Ruth, walked in the door, carrying bags from three local fabric shops. Debbie and Ruby exchanged a meaningful glance, then invited Ruth to join them in the living room.

"Please have a seat and join us, Mother." Debbie said, rising. "Can I offer you something to drink?"

The False Groom

Every person has a limit – and Annie Gates was well past hers. Her family and friends had taken advantage of her amenable disposition long enough, and Annie was going to take action. She wouldn't accept their mistreatment any longer.

Annie had been a second-class citizen in her own family ever since she was a child. She was bright, loving, and helpful, but those qualities had gotten her nowhere. She had a sweet, round face, pale skin, and ginger-colored curly hair. Her eyes were a warm, but unremarkable brown, and it was soon obvious that her parents were somewhat disappointed with her looks. They were a handsome couple and had expected stunning children.

When Lola was born two years after Annie, their dreams were realized. Lola had lush honey blonde hair, huge cornflower blue eyes, and a vivacious personality that demanded attention. Lola demanded, their parents gave, and Annie was relegated to the background – ignored. They didn't acknowledge her winning attributes, including her gentle spirit, her beautiful singing voice, or the pretty way about her.

Their most recent batch of letters had finally driven Annie over the edge. She hadn't seen her family or friends in over a year, since she'd left Chicago to travel to the teaching position she'd been offered in Lewiston, Idaho. The letters they traded back and forth were Annie's only link to her childhood home, her family, her roots. Annie was, of course, a faithful correspondent, sending a letter to her family weekly to help maintain family ties.

Dear Mother, Father, and Lola,

I hope this letter finds you all well and happy. How are things in Chicago? I'm sure you're enjoying nice weather by now — a much-needed respite from the deep freeze of winter. Thinking of the cold wind whipping off Lake Michigan takes me back to past Chicago winters and makes me shiver as I write this note at the little desk in my room, sitting in a warm patch of afternoon sun. I suppose one's bones never forget such an incredible chill!

All is well here in Lewiston and in my classroom. I wish I had a photograph of my one-room schoolhouse. It's so quaint — like nothing I'd ever seen in Chicago. My students can be a bit restless in the morning and sleepy in the afternoon, so I have them sing several times throughout the day. You know how I love to sing, and the children do too. It seems to calm them when they're antsy and lift them when their energy is flagging. Overall, I've seen great improvement in academic performance since I started here last year. At times it still seems a bit odd to be in such a rural area. I do miss the hustle and bustle of the city at the oddest moments…

I'll sign off for now so I can get this over to the post office. I'll write a longer letter next week. I hope to hear from you soon.

Love,
Annie

The incoming letters were far more sporadic. Annie was surprised if she received more than one letter per month. They made sure to write when Lola became engaged though – in fact, they'd all written then. None of their letters asked how Annie was doing, but they went on at length about

Lola's big news. Annie's mother wrote:

> *Your father and I couldn't be happier with Lola's intended. He's exactly the kind of young man we'd like associated with the family. We didn't count on you getting married, of course, and so our hopes rested on your sister. Naturally it was just a matter of time before someone asked for her hand. However, the reality of the situation is even better than we'd hoped for. His family is quite wealthy and well connected.*

Annie had never known her mother to be tactful or terribly kind, so her words weren't shocking but they were disappointing.

Soon after receiving news of the engagement, Annie sent a letter to Lola and her parents, wishing her sister all the best in life and love and offering her sincere congratulations on the engagement. She also repeated an earlier invitation for them to come visit her in Lewiston so they could see where she lived and worked. After all, they had the means to come visit, and it would be nice to see her family, such as they were.

Lola replied to her letter rather quickly by her family's standards, saying that - although she appreciated Annie's best wishes - she and their parents were shocked at Annie's selfish behavior.

> *How can you possibly expect us to travel to the far reaches of the country when we've got a wedding to plan? Perhaps your lack of experience in matters of love have left you without a frame of reference for what one does during an engagement period, but there is much to be done here before the wedding. We couldn't possibly break away from these crucial preparations for a jaunt to the country. I'm sure you understand, dear sister.*

Annie knew Lewiston was "out in the sticks" compared to Chicago. Indeed, her family's dining room was nearly as big as the schoolhouse where she taught in town. But that wasn't the point. True to form, Annie responded that of course she understood the wedding would require a lot of preparation and she'd just plan on seeing them when she traveled back to Chicago for the wedding. Her father had next responded in his squatty handwriting.

Dear Annie,
Please find enclosed a copy of your sister's engagement announcement. We just hosted an engagement party for the bride- and groom-to-be. It was at the County Club, and the party was a smashing success.

Mother, Lola, and I discussed your trip back home for the wedding and decided it would be utterly unfair to ask you to travel such a long way to attend. It's unlikely you'd even be allowed to take time off in the middle of the term. We'll be sure to send you photographs and tell you all about it. The Chicago Daily News *will undoubtedly do a write-up; we'll send it along as soon as we're able.*

He had signed off shortly after that, having fulfilled his purpose. Again Annie was put aside, considered an unnecessary distraction and summarily dismissed. Annie didn't immediately respond to his letter - she was rolling the series of letters around in her mind, contemplating the recent turn of events and the consistent neglect she'd endured over the years.

The final straw was the letter Annie received from one of her school "friends." Mary Evans was the daughter of Annie's mother's best friend, Linda Chester. Although they'd never been close, Annie maintained the correspondence with Mary after she'd moved to Idaho out of respect for family ties dating back to when both girls were infants. Mary often wrote effusive letters detailing the joys of her married life, lamenting that Annie wasn't able to experience the same joys that she herself had been blessed with. In the past, she'd expressed hope Annie would marry one day, adding there was "someone out there for everyone!"

In her most recent letter, Mary no longer seemed to be hopeful for Annie at all, although she didn't declare her an old maid outright – which was a comfort, given that Annie was a mere twenty years old. After gushing over Lola's engagement, fiancé, and upcoming nuptials, Mary wrote, "How wonderful that you've got all your little school children to nurture, since it seems unlikely you'll ever have children of your own."

Annie was not a mean, angry, or vindictive person. However, she knew what was right and wrong, and knew she was being treated poorly. She wasn't sure why her family members and those in their social circle felt it was acceptable to be so rude and thoughtless. They seemed to think that tact wasn't required if they were telling the truth – at least the truth as they saw it. Annie was reminded for the thousandth time that wealth, breeding, and social standing had nothing to do with manners and class.

Annie questioned herself for one brief moment: Was she doing something to bring this upon herself? After reflecting on her life in Lewiston, she knew it wasn't her. It truly was her family. Thirteen months ago, when she'd moved to a new town – a new state – where she didn't know a soul, she'd been immediately welcomed. She had been treated with kindness and respect by her students' families and the community at large and had been invited to participate in nearly every social activity in town – even if she wasn't invited to be an integral part in her own sister's wedding.

Annie was a gifted teacher, so it was no wonder she was welcomed with open arms. She made learning fun and engaged even the most reluctant students. She dealt with the occasional discipline problem in the best possible way: She was firm, calm, and fair. If a student seemed to be acting out or having problems, she gave him or her extra attention and made every effort to get the student back on a solid course, instead of simply writing the student off as a troublemaker.

Annie attended church regularly and sang in the choir. Her lovely soprano voice was easy to pick out and was clearly the best of all the women in the choir. She was humble though and, when any compliment was paid, she demurred and said she was just one person, trying to contribute to the greater good and express her devotion through song.

Annie was in church the Sunday after receiving Mary Evans' letter when she decided to proceed with a morally questionable course of action. The craziest of ideas had popped into her mind the night before while she had been mending stockings by lamplight in her room. She'd quickly dismissed the idea as too outlandish and dishonest. However, when the pastor wrapped up his sermon by reminding the congregation that the Lord helps those who help themselves, Annie became convinced by his words. She knew what she was planning was most certainly a sin, yet she also knew it was high time she helped herself – to a sense of satisfaction.

The first part of her plan was to halt any correspondence with her family. She'd be writing them soon enough. Next, she had to create a stunning wedding outfit. Annie went down to the general store and visited Mrs. Marshall, who was in charge of the fabric and notions. Annie purchased some velvet, decorative trim, tulle, buttons, and flowers – supplies to create a beautiful dress and veil. Mrs. Marshall wanted to know what Annie was making with the materials, and Annie tried to be as vague as possible while still being truthful, saying, "It's for a project I'm working on for my family."

"Oh, well, it's lovely fabric, Miss Gates. I'm sure it will be beautiful when it's done – whatever it is."

Mrs. Marshall was a bit of a busybody, and Annie knew her curiosity was piqued. She took her leave before Mrs. Marshall could ask any more questions.

Annie spent a considerable amount of time making the skirt, the fitted jacket, and the veil and was immensely pleased with the results. The dark rust colored velvet went nicely with her coloring. It was the perfect ensemble for a wedding in the ruggedly beautiful surroundings of Lewiston, and it fit like a glove. Annie was ready to proceed with the next part of her plan – the part that would start tongues in town wagging, if they hadn't already begun.

Cecil Calhoun was a handsome devil and was widely considered the handsomest man in town – at least by those who were attracted to scoundrels. He certainly wasn't Annie's type, but she didn't need an actual husband, just a false groom who'd look good for the camera when they had their "wedding portrait" taken. Annie knew she was risking her job by even speaking with the man, but moved forward with her plan anyway. She'd show her mother, her father, Lola, and Mary – all of them.

Annie arranged through a third party for Cecil to meet her in Lewiston's only restaurant. She certainly couldn't pop into the saloon he frequented, so she sent a messenger in her place. The peculiar request – to meet the virtuous schoolmarm – would surely be too interesting to be ignored. Indeed, he showed up at the appointed time. Annie introduced herself, holding her hand out for a proper handshake, then pitched her plan, laying out his potential involvement.

"I'm sure this will seem quite odd to you, Mr. Calhoun, but I'd like to hire you. I'm playing a practical joke of sorts and need a handsome man to stand in as my groom in a photographic portrait. It would only require one hour of your time, on a day to be mutually agreed upon, and I would pay you for your modeling services."

Cecil Calhoun was leaning back in his wooden chair as he stared rakishly at Annie. He wasn't sure what the schoolteacher was up to, but he admired her for meeting his gaze steadily – and for not treating him with the obvious disdain that some of the other churchgoers in town did. He had quite a reputation as a ladies' man, a gambler, and a drinker. To associate with him at any level was a risk for someone in her position. Impressed and intrigued, he decided to work with her as requested. She must want this photo pretty bad. Why not line his pocket with a bit of cash and help her at the same time?

"Sure, I'll help you Miss Gates." He winked at her, just for fun.

Annie went on as if she hadn't seen it. "Thank you, Mr. Calhoun. Let's meet next Saturday at noon at the portrait studio down the street, if that works for you. Please come well groomed and wearing your best suit. I'll provide your boutonnière."

They agreed upon a price for his participation, and Annie promised to provide the cash after the photograph was taken. Schoolteacher Annie Gates said a polite goodbye and walked out of the restaurant, nervous but determined.

The following Saturday Cecil Calhoun was at the studio at noon as promised. When he saw Annie emerge from the changing room with her wedding attire on, fluffing the veil, he said, "What a nice dress, Miss Gates."

Mr. Baker, the photographer, couldn't contain himself any longer. "I had no idea the two of you were a couple, let alone newly married!"

"Oh no, Mr. Baker, this photograph is quite staged, I assure you," Annie said quickly. "I'm playing a bit of a practical joke on my family, you see. Mr. Calhoun is just standing in as the groom today." Annie tried to look calm, as if the situation were perfectly reasonable and required no further explanation. It seemed to work.

Mr. Baker mumbled a quiet "I see" and went about posing them, although he didn't understand at all and wondered what kind of a joke involved a false groom – especially when the groom was the nefarious Cecil Calhoun. After snapping the photograph, Mr. Baker saw the exchange of money and found it most peculiar, although it made sense under the conditions Annie Gates had described.

Annie ordered a handful of copies of the photograph Mr. Baker had snapped of the "newlyweds." When they were ready, she sat down to write the letters to her family and Mary Evans. The letter to her family was the longer of the two, and Annie took immense pleasure in writing it. She'd outlined what she would include and was tickled with the results.

> *Dear Mother, Father, and Lola,*
> *I hope this letter finds you all well and happy. I also hope the wedding plans are progressing well. As it turns out, I've got some news of my own. I almost didn't bother to write, for fear of being accused of stealing Lola's thunder or distracting the three of you from your all-consuming preparations, but in the end I decided to write so you could at least send any future correspondence addressed in the right name. My married name is Annie Anderson.*
>
> *Yes, I've recently been married! My husband's name is Erik Anderson - and what a whirlwind romance we've had. We both attend the same church here in town, which is where we met, and Erik said he first noticed me because of my singing voice. He calls me his little Songbird – isn't that the sweetest thing? We'd only been dating for a short while when he proposed. Erik said he knew it was meant to be from the very first, and I couldn't resist and said yes immediately.*

We had the loveliest wedding in our church, and the ladies in the choir, with whom I sing every Sunday, helped decorate with loads of gorgeous blooms from their gardens. Erik's mother, Irene, is quite a talented baker, and she made us the most exquisite cake ever. It was better looking and more delicious than any of cakes served at Chicago's society weddings, if I may say so. Making our cake was an act of love, not necessity, as Erik comes from a well-to-do family here in Idaho. They've made their fortune in logging, and Erik will likely take over the business when his father retires. Mr. and Mrs. Anderson are such kind, loving people. I feel blessed to have been welcomed so warmly into such an exceptional family.

Based on our past correspondence and your most recent letters, I didn't bother to send invitations to the wedding. I knew you couldn't be bothered to trek out here - that you're so very busy. In place of an invitation, I'm sending this letter and a portrait taken on our wedding day. Isn't Erik a handsome devil? I just know we'll have beautiful children — he hopes to have at least six. I've also tucked in some pressed rose petals from my bouquet.

I must sign off now, dear family. Please know that Erik and I will be living here in Lewiston, and I don't anticipate a return to Chicago. However, I wish you all the best in the years to come.

Sincerely,
Annie Anderson

Annie was prepared for shock, disbelief, scorn, wrath — or whatever else they might send her way, including no response at all. When she'd set her plan in motion, she had prepared herself to cut ties with her family forever. It wasn't as if she'd be missing out on anything by doing so, except maybe some well-placed daggers to the heart.

She bundled together the letter, the photograph, and the pressed flower petals and addressed the envelope to her family in Chicago. She put the name Annie Anderson on the return address and did the same on the envelope she addressed to Mary Evans, which contained similar contents. After handing over the letters for mailing, Annie brushed her hands together as if she was knocking off some annoying dirt or dust and turned to go about the rest of her life.

Truth be told, she had a lingering feeling of nervousness that she would receive some grand punishment for her rebellious act. Instead, was gifted with a Mr. Simon Tobin.

Simon was the bookkeeper at the large general store in town and had in fact noticed Miss Annie Gates at church. Every time she sang a solo in her sweet, clear voice, his heart pounded in his chest. He'd been watching her for some time. Although he'd been drawn to her from the start, it took him months to work up the nerve to speak to her. He was quite shy. Finally, after services one Sunday after she'd "married" the fictitious Erik Anderson, he approached her on the church steps.

"Hello, Miss Gates. My name is Simon Tobin."

"Hello, Mr. Tobin, I'm pleased to meet you." Annie was familiar with Simon's name and face, although they'd never actually spoken.

"I hope you don't mind me saying so, but you've got the most beautiful singing voice. I've never heard anything quite so lovely. It's truly uplifting." He tried not to blush as he spoke, knowing how earnest he sounded.

Annie modestly replied, "Thank you kindly, Mr. Tobin. I'm pleased to sing with the choir as part of our weekly service."

Simon took a deep breath and said, "I was wondering if you might accompany me on a picnic next Saturday. Mrs. Locke, with whom I board, makes the most delicious lunches, and I'd be happy to order a basket lunch for us to share. I know of a lovely spot down by the river…." His voice trailed off uncertainly.

Surprised, Annie quickly regained her composure and said graciously, "I'd be delighted, Mr. Tobin. Thank you for the invitation."

Releasing a silent sigh of relief, Simon asked Annie if he could walk her home from church; when she accepted, he offered his arm. They chatted amiably during the walk and arranged to picnic at noon the following Saturday.

Simon was right. Mrs. Locke was an excellent cook and was quite generous when she packed the picnic basket for Simon. Excited that one of her favorite boarders had a date, she provided a veritable feast. The basket was filled to the brim with ham sandwiches, potato salad, flaky biscuits, fresh berries, sugar cookies, and two mason jars filled with chilled sweet tea.

Annie and Simon sat on a blanket near the river and enjoyed their meal, visiting between bites. Both tried to eat as neatly as possible to make a good impression. After they'd finished, Simon admitted to Annie that he'd been interested in her for some time. Annie was flattered, but her heart was heavy. She felt she had to come clean with Simon knowing she wasn't exactly who he thought she was.

"Simon, you seem like a wonderful man, and I'm so flattered that you've expressed interest in me. However, I have to be honest and tell you something quite shocking. I'm already married, and am not as moral as I might seem."

Simon's eyes widened a bit at her news, but when he asked her to explain and drew the whole story out of her, he understood. When she summed up the recent events – the "joke" she'd played on her family - she finished by saying,

"I'm not terribly proud of what I did, but I'm not terribly sorry either. I was tired of being treated like a second-class citizen by those who were supposed to love me the most. I'll understand if you find my behavior unacceptable."

Simon smiled and put Annie's fears to rest. "I'm actually not as surprised as you might think. There was some talk in town; folks wondered what was going on. Your meetings with Cecil Calhoun worked the local gossips up into a fine frenzy, and there was concern given that you're the town's schoolteacher. However, in the end it was decided that as there was no evidence of any actual wrongdoing, nothing would be said to you. You're the best teacher we've ever had, and no one wanted to ruin things for the kids. That doesn't mean folks weren't mighty curious though!"

Annie and Simon talked some more, there by the river, and forged a bond that endured for the rest of their lives. Miss Annie Gates soon became Mrs. Simon Tobin, and they had a lovely wedding. The members of their church pitched in, and ladies from the choir helped to decorate the church. They also made Annie's bouquet from the flowers in their gardens. Mrs. Locke, with whom Simon had boarded for so long, gave Annie and Simon the gift of an exquisite cake – more beautiful and delicious than anything Annie had ever seen in the big city of Chicago, and Annie pressed some of the petals from her bridal bouquet as a keepsake.

The newlyweds moved into a charming cottage-style house that Simon bought with money he'd saved by living frugally and managing his money wisely. Annie and Simon planned on having children and hoped to stay on in Lewiston indefinitely. As they got settled into bed one night, shortly after their wedding, husband and wife looked at each other. The kerosene lamp flickered and light danced through the room.

"Are you happy, Mrs. Tobin?"

"Yes, I'm quite happy Mr. Tobin! There's only one thing missing from our wedding ceremony and recent union."

"What's that, Mrs. Tobin?" Simon wanted to provide everything that his little songbird's heart desired.

Annie gave her husband a mischievous grin. "I was thinking we should make an appointment with Mr. Baker to have our wedding portrait taken. Don't you agree?"

Beatrice Buttons

Not everyone is called to live in the ethereal netherworld, where the past joins the present. Where what was merges with what is, while what could have been swirls around constantly like a thick, cloying mist scented with melancholy and bittersweet. Most people don't have to live there, and many aren't even aware such a place exists. It's incredibly real though, as anyone who has experienced loss or trauma in his or her young life can tell you.

Beatrice lived in this netherworld for years before moving out into the bright light that shines where the present gives way to the future. She wasn't consulted before she was shuttled off to this netherworld, damp with what wasn't, it just happened when her mother died. She was nearly four when her mother died in childbirth, taking Beatrice's nearly born baby sister with her. Beatrice had just enough memories of her mother, Iris, to miss her desperately in the time immediately following her death and for years afterwards.

Beatrice had always been a quiet and shy child. For months after her mother died, Beatrice was nearly mute. Her father, not knowing how to get through to her, did the only thing he could think of: He remarried. Naturally Beatrice didn't see this as an act of loyalty or as the best way to preserve the memory of her mother, but her father did have her best interest at heart. Grant Sutton knew he wasn't equipped to raise a child alone and that Beatrice needed a mother, so he carefully chose someone who would love the child as her own. Not all stepchildren are so lucky, as most anyone – including the fabled Cinderella – will agree.

Audrey Sutton was a sweet and nurturing soul, and her heart ached for the motherless Beatrice. She did all she could to bond with the emotionally wispy child. Unfortunately, all too soon, Audrey had to balance Beatrice with the steady progression of children she bore to her husband. It seemed Audrey just had to walk into the same room as Grant in order to conceive, so Beatrice wasn't an only child for long.

By the time Audrey gave birth to what would be their last child, Audrey and Grant had had four girls and three boys together, making Beatrice the eldest of eight. Beatrice was part of the family, but she could never forget that it wasn't entirely her family. Her mother, half of where Beatrice had come from, lay buried in the cemetery on the outskirts of town. Beatrice sometimes wondered if her mother had taken part of her with her when she'd died.

Her stepmother, Audrey, had been thoughtful enough to pack Iris' possessions away for Beatrice to enjoy when she was older. One day, when the little girl seemed especially blue, Audrey took her to the attic and showed her the trunk containing these treasures. Among the dresses, aprons, and other personal items was a bag of buttons. It was a cloth bag made of thick off-white cotton with a built-in drawstring, and it was filled with buttons that had been used on Iris's clothes. Functional ornamentation wasn't discarded when an item of clothing was no longer wearable; it was removed and saved for the next garment. These buttons were all awaiting placement on a new piece of clothing when Iris died.

Beatrice was fascinated with the buttons and quietly asked her stepmother if she could have them, her downcast eyes filled with hope and yearning.

"Of course you can have them, Beatrice. One day you'll be given all your mother's things, but your father decided you should get them when you're older. I think the buttons are a nice keepsake for you in the meantime." Audrey Sutton smiled at Beatrice and gave her a quick hug before guiding her back downstairs.

Beatrice, still mired in the netherworld, hung on to the buttons fiercely, as if they were tiny life preservers instead of shaped bits of mother-of-pearl. She carried the small bag of buttons everywhere and loved to imagine the garments they'd been attached to as well as the things her mother might've done while wearing them. Over time she developed a different story for each and every button in the bag, with her mother playing the role of the central character in each story. Beatrice would play with the buttons for hours, laying them out in careful patterns to create shapes and spell out words. She was rarely seen without her tiny treasures - so much so that her father began to call her Beatrice Buttons, which made the girl smile and giggle every time.

When Beatrice was nearly twelve she sewed a new blouse for the first time, guided by her Grandma Sutton, who was a talented seamstress and a patient teacher. Beatrice incorporated seven of Iris' buttons in her design. Excited to have made something by herself and to have incorporated her mother's buttons, Beatrice was awash with emotion as she sewed the last button on. With each stitch and each breath, she realized she herself was like the very garment she held in her hands. The blouse was comprised of different pieces, stitched together to form a whole, and so was Beatrice. She felt as though a third of her young life was bound to a woman she now struggled to remember: her cherished mother. The remaining two-thirds were tied up in her life with her father, her stepmother, and her brothers and sisters. In her mind's eye, she could almost see the seam that ran the length of her, the sideways stitches and ivory thread that held the formative pieces of her together. Beatrice wondered if she'd ever feel whole, as if woven into one piece of cloth.

The Suttons celebrated Beatrice's twelfth birthday with a small family party on a Saturday afternoon. The lunch menu featured Beatrice's favorite foods: fried chicken with mashed potatoes, fresh corn on the cob, and Audrey's spectacular melt-in-your-mouth biscuits topped with honey butter. Dessert was a towering white layer cake topped with a fluffy white icing interspersed with layers of fresh strawberries. They'd all enjoyed the delicious lunch and were savoring slices of cake when Mike, the sibling nearest in age to Beatrice who was sitting directly to her left, starting pestering her.

"What did you wish for, Beatrice?" Mike nudged her as he asked, poking her side with his right elbow.

Beatrice remained silent and calmly ate her cake. She knew she couldn't share her birthday wish or it wouldn't come true.

Mike seemed to care very little about the rules associated with birthday wishes and elbowed her side again. "What did you wish for, Beatrice?"

More silence, but Beatrice was getting annoyed – both with his poking and his verbal prodding.

"Tell me what you wished for Beatrice!" Mike insisted with a final and more forceful elbow to the side. Grant and Audrey Sutton, who had been talking with the adults at the other end of the table, shifted their attention to the two children just as Mike was launching his final assault on the birthday girl. Grant was a second away from telling his son to stop bothering Beatrice when she handled it herself.

In all her twelve years, Beatrice had never raised her voice. She'd never fought with her brothers or sisters and had always been a kind helper when Audrey needed an extra set of hands. So when she angrily shoved her chair back, stood, slammed her fork down on the dining table, and shouted "I wished that I'd had more time with my mother!" at the top of her lungs, the family barely recognized her.

Mike, insensitive boy that he was, muttered, "That's not the kind of thing you're supposed to wish for – something in the past. You're supposed to wish for a toy or something."

Beatrice glared at him angrily for two beats, her face flushed red, then bolted from the table and ran for the back door.

Grant Sutton asked his parents to watch the other children while he and Audrey went after Beatrice, seeking her out in her favorite spot in the backyard. She was sitting on the swing that dangled from the huge oak tree, swaying to and fro as if stirred by the gentlest of breezes. She had tears rolling down her cheeks, and her hands loosely held the cloth bag of buttons so dear to her heart. Beatrice turned toward her father and Audrey as they approached. "I'm sorry to have shouted at my birthday party. It was so nice, and I ruined it."

"You didn't ruin a thing, Beatrice; you just spoke up for yourself. There's no shame in that." Audrey's voice was soothing and she gestured for Beatrice to sit between them on the grass near the swing. Beatrice joined them, hiccupping slightly as her tears lingered.

Grant reached out his hand to his eldest daughter. "I'm so sorry you lost your mother so young, sweetie. Iris was an amazing woman, and I still miss her. When I proposed to Audrey, I made sure to tell her that I'd always love your mother, and she understood that. I looked for a woman to help raise you, for I knew you needed a mother as well as a father, and I know Audrey loves you as much as she loves your brothers and sisters." He met Audrey's eyes in silent thanks before continuing.

"Is there anything we can do to help you with the loss you still feel, Beatrice?" he asked. "We love you, and want to do anything we can to help. Losing a parent can be like living with an empty well inside, and perhaps that well can never be filled. But if it can be filled, and we're just not giving what you need, we hope you'll let us know."

Beatrice was silent for a moment, ashamed that her outburst had caused doubt and concern that their parenting skills were lacking in some way. She assured them it was nothing that they had or hadn't done; it was just a feeling that she walked around with. "Sometimes I feel like the well you mentioned, daddy - like there's something missing, and no matter how much love and attention you've each given me, I'm still missing the one person who's not here, who can never be here."

As she looked at her parents and saw the worry in their faces, Beatrice had a revelation. She realized that, although she'd always miss the idea of her mother and would be a bit nostalgic for what could've been had her mother lived, her preoccupation with that first third of her life was keeping her from fully embracing the many blessings in her life now. It was a mature concept for a twelve-year-old to grasp, but it was suddenly very clear.

Years later, when Beatrice looked back on her life, she pinpointed that twelfth birthday as the day she moved away from the vague netherworld of what wasn't into the shining sun of what was and what could be. She knew that her perception was the all-important sun shining high in the sky. If she chose to be present and appreciative, her life would be full, warm, and dry - whether or not storms threatened or occasionally settled in.

Beatrice eventually became a mother and had two sons and three daughters of her own. When they asked about her mother, she told them about both of her mothers: Audrey, who had raised her, and Iris, who had given birth to her. She showed them the buttons she'd adored so much as a child, and they were astonished to find there was an entire story wrapped up in every single button. They took turns picking buttons and loved hearing all the Grandma Iris stories as Beatrice unraveled the tales she'd woven so many years ago. There was only joy in telling these stories now, for somewhere over the years, after that twelfth birthday, Beatrice began to feel as though she was whole – as if she had been woven into one contiguous piece of cloth.

And Some for the Road

Savannah had always lived a peculiar existence. She was born into slavery and adopted into freedom. She was neither colored nor white, really, because of the unusual situation she'd been raised in. She couldn't relate to most colored people because of her experiences and upbringing and, although she was raised in a white family, she was still a woman of color – something Savannah and those around her could never forget.

Though the details of her first months would always be a mystery to Savannah and those who raised her, she'd been born to the slave cook of a wealthy plantation owner in Georgia. She was orphaned by her mother's sudden death when she was nearly two. A female relative cared for her for a short period of time, but the day the woman was sold at auction Savannah was left alone with the other "stock," crying frantically in the enclosure in which the slaves were locked until it was their turn on the auction block.

James and Sarah Forrester, Northern Quakers passing through the area, saw the little girl. Their hearts broke to see her alone and distressed. Sarah made a split-second decision, turning to James to say quietly and firmly, "I want that child. We'll raise her as our daughter." James, looking deeply into his wife's eyes, nodded his assent. They'd arrived as a childless couple and would leave with a daughter - as a family.

Although James was a quiet and calm man, he was a determined negotiator. Sarah's eyes were wet with tears as the toddler continued to cry, and she was horrified to think of the child's fate should James not succeed in buying her freedom. Sarah needn't have worried. James motioned her over, smiling, and Sarah rushed to the little girl. As she picked up the crying child, Sarah realized how soggy they both were – from the warmth of the fierce Georgia sun and from the tears soaking the front of the girl's loose, threadbare shift. Sarah drew the child close, chest against chest, and felt the heat and humidity seal them together. She knew from that instant that they were bonded for life. The girl quieted quickly and, exhausted from her ordeal, was soon asleep in Sarah Forrester's arms.

As the Forresters made the long journey home to Rhode Island with their new charge, they marveled at the twists of fate that had led them to their new daughter. James had business in Savannah, Georgia, and Sarah had accompanied him as the couple was unwilling to be apart for the duration of such a long journey. On the day they found their daughter, they'd needed to send a telegraph and had happened upon the spectacle of the slave auction on the way to the office. The Forresters were abolitionists who believed in equality of both race and gender, and they had been horrified at the human tragedy that had unfolded before them: the incomprehensible act of one human being sold to another, families being torn apart. Seeing the abandoned little girl had been too much for their hearts to bear.

James told Sarah about his negotiations, that the auctioneer wanted to put the orphaned girl up on the auction block like the other slaves. He planned to start the bidding at $500, although a lone child wasn't nearly as saleable as one with a family to care for it was. James offered him $500 right away, but when the auctioneer threatened to put the child up in the hopes of getting even more James jumped up to $600 immediately and the deal was sealed.

Sarah smiled at James as he recounted his story, and murmured, "It's the best $600 we've ever spent. Since we don't know what this precious child's birth name is, why don't we name her Savannah? We don't know anything about her origins, but this name – after the city where we all came together – can be one little reminder." That's how Savannah Cecilia Forrester got her name – and new parents.

While Savannah was getting settled in at their home in Rhode Island, James Forrester started the process of adoption, so he and Sarah would legally be her parents. He wrote an ironclad will that designated Savannah as their sole heir and made sure the papers verifying her freedom were in order. They put copies of all these documents in a safe deposit box at the bank in town. James and Sarah knew that it was essential to be thorough. Rhode Island was a free state, but that wouldn't keep a bounty hunter from snatching up free coloreds that could be falsely claimed as slaves. If papers documenting free status were lost or destroyed, the colored person in question might have no choice but to be forced into servitude. There were few victories when the word of a white man was pitted against the word of a falsely imprisoned Negro. The Forresters kept Savannah close by at all times for that very reason and had multiple copies of all essential documents as a precaution.

Happily, their new child settled in well. When she was young she called Sarah "mama" and James "papa." When she was older - old enough to know she was different and that they'd adopted her - she called them Mother Forrester and Father Forrester, or just Mother and Father. She knew they were the only parents she'd ever have and was lucky to have them, but Savannah also knew she'd started her life far away from Rhode Island, with a different mother and father.

The Forresters raised her exactly the same way they would've raised one of their biological children, if they'd been blessed with any. From the time she was five, Savannah received formal schooling from her father. He'd work with her from eight until noon, teaching her all that she would've learned at school – and more. Academics were carefully taught, as was self-defense. James and Sarah Forrester were peace-loving people, but they were realistic when it came to the ways of the world. James taught Savannah how to shoot and how to defend herself in a hand-to-hand situation as well.

After her morning studies with her father, Savannah would break for the noon meal with her family. When they'd finished eating, James Forrester would go to his office in town, where he practiced law, and Savannah would do homework or study for another hour.

Savannah's afternoons were spent on her domestic studies. Sarah was in charge of this part of her daughter's development, although she was equally qualified to teach Savannah's academics. Sarah wanted their child to be well rounded – intelligent and learned and able to do everything necessary to run a household. The Forresters had a woman on staff, Minnie, who helped with the housework, but they didn't want Savannah to grow up being waited on. They wanted her to be able to survive and thrive no matter what situations came her way, so Minnie didn't wait on young mistress Savannah. Minnie helped with Savannah's domestic instruction and was simply an extra set of hands around the Forrester home.

Savannah learned to cook, clean, bake, do the wash, and iron. She learned how to grow fruits and vegetables as well as how to can them. She learned how to care for the livestock and how to kill a chicken; she also learned how to chop and split wood. She was a hard worker and a quick learner who made the Forresters proud.

Savannah learned to do just about everything, yet it was only natural that she had her favorite tasks – as well as others she didn't enjoy quite as much. She showed early aptitude for sewing and baking; indeed, baking soon stuck out as a God-given gift. Whether sweet or savory, all of Savannah's baked goods were delectable. By the time she was ten years old she was well known for her baking prowess and was constantly working to improve her skills and to expand her repertoire. James Forrester practically lived for Savannah's cornbread, and if he wasn't watched carefully he could eat a whole pan by himself. Slathered in butter and smeared with honey, it was one of his favorite treats.

Savannah excelled at baking functional fare like breads and biscuits, but she really loved to bake desserts. She created delectable fruit pies, soaring layer cakes, and rich puddings. Some of Savannah's most cherished hours were spent in the kitchen with Mother Forrester and Minnie, baking up a storm as she waited for Father Forrester to come home and sample the treats she'd made. Savannah tried new recipes and perfected existing recipes.

Her real specialty was baking cookies. Among her favorite cookie recipes were lemon jumbles, snickerdoodles, shortbread, macaroons, and soft iced apple cookies. She found she could even earn a bit of pocket money from baking, if she wished. Her cookies quickly drew a steady stream of customers wanting to purchase dozens at a time as they became available. The Forresters provided everything Savannah could ever need or want, but encouraged this bit of commerce so their daughter would better understand business, even if it was on such a small scale.

Around this same time, at the age of ten, the Forresters taught Savannah about the Underground Railroad. They'd been sure to teach her about slavery over the years, and she knew the story of how she'd been "specially chosen" at the auction now that she was a bit older, but this information about the Underground Railroad was new to her. Savannah was fascinated by this secret system that helped slaves escape to freedom and was thrilled to learn that their Quaker friends, Mr. and Mrs. Coates, were stationmasters. The Coates home was a station along the Underground Railroad's path north to Canada. Savannah was sworn to secrecy, and James and Sarah trusted that their responsible daughter would keep the information to herself – Savannah knew it was a matter of life and death to do so.

James and Sarah were also "stockholders" in the Underground Railroad, a term given to those who helped finance the operation. Soon their daughter was too. Around Savannah's eleventh birthday, which they celebrated on March 6th because they didn't know her exact date of birth, the Forresters took their young daughter to the Coates home to see one of the "passengers" – a slave who had arrived at the Coates "station" the night before. On impulse, Savannah took along a dozen of her freshly baked lemon jumbles – buttery and sweet ring-shaped cookies covered with a citrus glaze. When the Forrester family arrived at the Coates home, Savannah was allowed to see the secret room that sequestered the escaped slave traveling north. Mrs. Coates was delivering a meal to the understandably nervous woman they were sheltering, whose name was Sabine, and Savannah shyly followed Mrs. Coates into the room. Savannah had placed the lemon jumbles in a dish covered with a clean tea towel before they left home, and she drew the towel back to expose the cookies to their intended recipient. Sabine's eyes widened a bit at the sight of the cookies, and she started to reach a hand out, but withdrew it – as if she was afraid she'd be punished. Savannah quietly said, "It's okay, take one. All of these cookies are for you, Miss Sabine."

Savannah had never felt so good about her baking as she did when Sabine, whose body had been beaten and whose spirits seemed to be flagging, smiled in delight after tasting Savannah's cookie. She quickly ate another two cookies while young Savannah stood there; later, when Savannah and Mrs. Coates retrieved the dishes they'd left with Sabine so she could eat in peace, Savannah saw that all twelve of the lemon jumbles had been eaten. Not a crumb remained. Savannah regarded that as the most meaningful praise she could hope to receive and decided she'd bake for passengers of the Underground Railroad on a regular basis.

Whenever the Coates' had a runaway slave as a guest, Savannah would see they were treated to some of her cookies.

Back home, Savannah and her parents soon realized she'd have to be very cautious about the cookies she shared, lovely idea that it was. By now Savannah was known for baking certain kinds of cookies, and if a runaway slave was captured with any of the cookies in their possession, they might be traced back to young Miss Forrester, putting the family and the other local supporters of the Underground Railroad in danger. So they decided the cookies she took would have to be enjoyed by the guests while still at the Coates home. Her father suggested that she serve her more delicate and dainty cookies to the guests while they were at the station and that she develop a special, sturdier cookie that they could take on the road. This cookie recipe would be top secret, so that no one except those working with the Underground Railroad would know who had provided the sweets.

Savannah was invigorated by the challenge. She wanted something hardy that would travel well, something that was filling and nutritionally sound, and something that would also provide a dose of sweetness along a rough journey. She happened upon the idea of bar cookies while baking her father a pan of the much-loved cornbread. She was inspired as she filled the greased pan with batter. She shared her idea with Mother Forrester and Minnie, who were chatting as they prepared dinner.

"What if I made bar cookies, with dough pressed into a square pan and later cut into squares instead of each cookie being individually baked? I could include things like nuts and raisins so it would be packed with delicious ingredients that would also give the runaways strength and energy during their travels." Savannah's rich brown eyes shone with excitement.

"That sounds marvelous, Savannah! I'm sure you'll create something that's both practical and delectable." Mother Forrester beamed at her helpful and thoughtful daughter and thanked the Lord – again – for bringing her into their lives.

In the end, Savannah packed a whole lot of goodness into her secret cookies. She named them Savannah's Starlight Cookie Bars, since the runaway slaves had to travel at night. She imagined them eating her cookie bars by starlight as they moved toward freedom.

Savannah added an interesting and filling twist to the cookie bars by incorporating oats into the mix. The Forresters knew a local Scottish family who ate oats as a hot breakfast cereal, although others in their town scoffed at the idea. They'd say, "Who eats oats - aside from horses?" Open to new ideas, Savannah discovered the oats made a tasty breakfast when prepared with sugar, cinnamon, and a little milk. After several variations, she ended up with a final cookie recipe that included goodies like flour, oats, butter, sugar, cinnamon, nuts, and raisins. If they had chunks of chocolate on hand, Savannah would chop them up and put those in instead of the raisins - either way was delicious. The family agreed the recipe was a winner in both taste and function as the bars could easily be stowed in a sack by those traveling north without losing much of the cookie to crumbling.

In addition to delivering dainties to be eaten at the Coates home and providing some of Savannah's Starlight Cookie Bars for each "passenger" to take out on the road, Savannah started to donate the proceeds of her baking business to the Underground Railroad. It made her proud to know she was helping people escape the cruelties and humiliations of slavery. Savannah couldn't change the U.S. government's laws, but she did all she could to help out in the meantime.

As the years passed, Savannah grew from a precious and talented child to a beautiful young woman. She continued to live at home, happily, with her parents. She never dated, given her peculiar position. White men were certainly attracted to her, but marriage between blacks and whites was illegal. Savannah might have married a black man, but the sad truth was that she didn't feel comfortable around many of the black men she'd met. There was such a difference in their life experiences – even things like their speech patterns were different. Savannah had spent most of her time at the Forrester home over the years and that's where she stayed.

Rumblings of Southern secession reached Rhode Island, and the Forrester family did all they could to support the Northern war effort when the Civil War began in 1861. By the time the war ended in 1865 and the 13th amendment to the constitution abolished slavery, everyone was weary of war. Folks like the Forresters, who were Quakers, had longed for peace all along, but knew slavery was an evil that simply could not be tolerated. They'd helped to fight the slavery system for all those years through the Underground Railroad and were unspeakably gratified when they no longer had to call themselves abolitionists.

Savannah, no longer a young woman, was now fifty-eight. Her parents, Sarah and James, were now elderly and their health began to fail. Savannah, devoted daughter that she was, cared for them until they died in 1867 – one right after the other. Sarah passed first, then James followed a short time later. James Forrester had been healthy, aside from being somewhat frail from old age, and Savannah knew deep down that he died of a broken heart. He'd spent his last days wandering the house looking lost. When he passed away in his sleep, Savannah knew he'd left to rejoin his beloved wife. Savannah had them buried side by side on the property and took fresh flowers to their graves every other day.

So much had changed in the world and in Savannah's life in the space of two years. A great and terrible war had ended in freedom for colored people, and she'd lost the two people she'd lived with for as long as she could remember. The three Forresters were inextricably linked and, although Savannah knew her parents had lived long and full lives, she missed them terribly. For a time all she could do was numbly maintain the usual household routines she'd kept since she was a child: cooking, cleaning, baking, washing. Only now she did all these things for one, not for three.

When Savannah made a pan of cornbread, she nearly ruined the batter with the salt of her tears, she missed Father Forrester so much. When she baked the soft iced apple cookies that were Mother Forrester's favorites, she could barely choke one down her throat, it was so thick with pent up emotion. Savannah had a lot of time to think, and in that lonely and silent time she thought of the recipes she'd come to know and love so well – the ones she'd baked hundreds of times. Whom would she pass those recipes down to? She'd stayed with her parents for so long that she herself had never become a parent. She didn't regret her years with the loving and kind Forresters, but their departures had definitely left a gaping hole in Savannah's life.

Not one to sit still for very long, Savannah was at a loss for the first time in her life. Productive, efficient, energetic – all these words described Savannah. Even when she'd felt alone, singular, and torn, she'd always been active and had a sense of purpose about her days. Now, at nearly sixty-one years old, she had to decide what she was going to do with the rest of her life.

She opted to make a few changes, starting with taking on on a small staff at the Forrester residence. She'd had one hired hand that saw to the outdoor chores, but Savannah really needed more help. There was too much for one person to do, and she wasn't getting any younger. Her parents had left her quite a bit of money, and as Savannah lived simply and frugally she could certainly afford to hire a small staff. She thought she might hire a husband and wife team: The wife could work in the house, and the husband could take care of the heavier work and the animals. In the end, things didn't work out quite the way she'd planned, and Savannah got a lot more than she'd hoped for.

Savannah went into town on her birthday and had her picture taken – her first portrait ever. Although she'd later remark it looked as though she'd tasted something sour as the photo was snapped, she was pleased that her face was still remarkably unlined and her white hair was neatly arranged. As she was coming out of the photographer's studio, Savannah bumped into Lucy Coates. Lucy had married into the Coates family and had come to know Savannah and her parents well over the years. They chatted a while, and Savannah mentioned she was thinking of bringing on some help – perhaps a husband and wife team.

"I'm so glad I ran into you then. There's a new family in town looking for work, and they might be just what you're looking for. I met them at the general store and can send them out to your place this afternoon, if you'd like. The man of the family, Toby, is helping us repair a fence on our property, but it's a quick fix."

Savannah agreed and thanked Lucy for the referral before the two ladies parted ways with fond goodbyes. That afternoon Savannah heard a wagon pull up out in front of the house and went to the porch to greet the newcomers. A family of four was making their way up the path, and Savannah introduced herself. She invited the family to sit on the shady front porch before she disappeared inside to fetch some lemonade. When she returned and had served the beverages, along with some of her shortbread cookies, she invited the family to tell her about themselves.

The man of the group, who was near sixty if he was a day, spoke for them. "Well, ma'am, my name is Toby Starke, and this is my family. We were all owned by white folks down in Virginia. They had a plantation where they grew tobacco, and we were some of their house slaves. I was their butler and driver, and my daughter here was one of the maids." His speech was very similar to the educated whites Savannah had socialized with much of her life, except for the Southern accent she found so charming. When he gestured toward his daughter, she introduced herself as Nellie, and introduced her children as well: a boy named Marcus, who was ten, and a girl named Lily, who was seven. Nellie said the children's father had been killed during the war.

"We're hoping to find work that will provide both room and board. We can do all the work necessary to keep this place running. We're honest, hardworking people, Miss Forrester," Toby said.

Savannah had a good feeling about the family, and although it might've been impetuous, she hired them on the spot. The family would live in the house with her and would earn modest wages in addition to room and board. Savannah invited them to get settled in. As she sat and sipped a cup of tea later that evening, she knew she'd made the right decision. It was wonderful to have life in the house again.

They quickly settled into a routine. Nellie worked with Savannah in the house, and they visited amiably as they cooked, washed, ironed, and cleaned. Toby tended the animals, did the heaviest work in the garden, and maintained the buildings. The children, Marcus and Lily, helped with some of the cleaning and gardening while also helping their grandpa with the animals.

Circumstance had never allowed the children regular schooling, so they were thrilled when Savannah offered to teach them for a few hours a day. Sitting in the very room where she'd received her education from Father Forrester,

Savannah taught the eager children to read, write, and do arithmetic. She also taught them about history and art, and the bright children happily drank up every bit of knowledge she shared with them.

Marcus and Lily were also enthusiastic where Savannah's baked goods were concerned. They loved everything Savannah baked for the family, and both brother and sister became her apprentices in the kitchen. Savannah patiently showed them how to make all the recipes she'd perfected over the years, and the children were soon enjoying both the baking process and the resulting treats that they helped to make.

Meanwhile, Savannah and Toby developed a special bond. Although Toby remained formal and somewhat removed from Savannah at first, in deference to her role as his employer, Savannah soon insisted that he call her by her first name instead of "Miss Forrester." Savannah often sat on the front porch in the afternoon, shelling peas or snapping beans for dinner. One day, Toby had asked if he could help her. They sat next to each other, snapping the mountain of green beans in an awkward silence at first, but they gradually transitioned into a quiet conversation.

That first day they mostly talked about the weather, the farm, and what was for dessert that night. As the days passed, they started to become more comfortable with each other and shared stories about their lives. Toby told Savannah about his years on the plantation. He'd had it a bit better as a house slave, but it had still been a life of hard work, frustration, and heartbreak. His wife, Nellie's mother, had been sold when Nellie was just a girl, and they'd never seen or heard of her again. Savannah heard a slight tremor in Toby's voice when he shared that particular bit of information, and she kept her eyes on the peas she was shelling so he wouldn't see the sympathy shining in her unshed tears.

Overcome with guilt, Savannah was initially reluctant to talk about her life. She too had been born a slave, but her life had been entirely different – and in many ways better – than what the Starke family had gone through. Toby was curious though and peppered her with enough questions that she finally opened up. She told him how her adopted mother and father had rescued her from the auction block and gave her everything they had. She told him about the quiet and simple life they lived – how she'd lived in the same house ever since she could remember.

Savannah shared that, although she was very thankful for her life and her many blessings, she'd always felt different. She wasn't white, but was socialized as though she were. She had black skin, but hadn't lived as most blacks had. It was as if she was caught somewhere in between, living in a world that was uniquely her own. Savannah was finally able to admit, as their hands busily worked, that - although her world had been a very nice one - it could also be a very lonely one.

Toby, who had a compassionate heart and didn't begrudge Savannah her good fortune, turned to her and smiled tenderly. "We all have our challenges and sorrows, don't we? You had freedom, but lacked a feeling of belonging. I felt like I belonged on the plantation, although I hated it. I know many of my living relatives and could honestly do without some of them while you probably wish you'd known your mama and daddy and likely wonder what they looked like."

Toby gently placed his hand over the top of Savannah's hand, where it had paused in the bowl of greens. "I've been alive for sixty-two years, and so much of what I've seen doesn't make any sense. Only God knows why things happen the way they do. All I know is that I have to keep moving forward and do the best I can each day. It's clear that's what you're doing too, Savannah. Your life hasn't been perfect, but you've made the best of things – and seem to have been a helpful and loving person since you were a child."

Savannah struggled to take in Toby's words. She was feeling so much all at once and was overcome with emotion to know that this man understood her, accepted her, and valued her. On a more primal level, Savannah's body was awash with excitement. Despite being a chaste touch, the feeling of Toby's hand on hers had set her blood to rushing through her veins. Her heart was thudding violently in her chest, and Savannah was afraid it was loud enough for Toby to hear.

Savannah quickly squeezed Toby's hand and murmured, "Thank you for your kindness and understanding, dear Toby. Please excuse me for a moment." She fled to her bedroom to compose herself and returned to the porch a few minutes later acting as if nothing was out of the ordinary.

As for Toby, he was now certain that he loved Savannah. He'd always respected her, enjoyed her company, and found her attractive. Their brief physical contact in the bowl of greens confirmed their physical chemistry – at least from Toby's point of view. How should he proceed? He had to tread carefully since it was a bit out of the ordinary to court one's employer, but in the end that's what he did. He started by asking her if she'd like to take a walk one evening and proposed a few months later when the family had gathered for supper.

He waited until they'd finished eating their meal and were about to have dessert. Nellie was bringing over a plate of snickerdoodles and a pot of tea when Toby asked Savannah to marry him. Marcus and Lily froze and sat wide-eyed and silent – each feverishly praying Savannah would say yes. When Savannah accepted with a girlish smile and said, "Yes, I'll marry you Toby," the room erupted in celebration and excited chatter. Savannah realized then that they were already a family.

After their simple wedding ceremony, a few changes were made to the household - namely Savannah and Toby moving into the master bedroom that had stood empty since her parents had passed. They'd prepared the room with a fresh coat of paint and a few other personal touches to make it their own, and the new husband and wife settled in. Savannah, who'd lain alone in bed every night, finally had passion in her life.

On the day she and Toby became engaged, their employment arrangement had ceased to exist, and their new family life had begun. A singular and only child who'd lived in the most peculiar circumstances finally felt at home with people aside from those who had adopted her. In one fell swoop, Savannah had gained a husband, a daughter, and two grandchildren. Savannah felt complete, now that she had others with whom to share her collection of recipes and her home – others with whom to share her life.

A Different Kind of Love

It had taken Ambrose a long time to accept himself for who he was. He suspected that his mother had known he was different all along, although they never spoke of the most shocking manifestation of this difference. In the end, he knew she approved of him and always wished the best for him, whatever that might be.

His mother, Gretchen, had seen the differences in him from a young age. Ambrose's older brothers, twins Stewart and Gilbert, were rambunctious, energetic, and bent on destruction. They constantly fought, jumped off things like furniture and porches, and were sweaty and grimy within minutes of climbing out of a bathtub. Meanwhile, Ambrose was calm and even-tempered, got a panicked look on his face when the twins roughhoused, and was likely to change his clothes immediately if he got dirty. Stewart and Gilbert had soon labeled Ambrose a mama's boy as he was often glued to Gretchen's side, but neither mother nor son cared what they thought or said.

Gretchen loved her precious little boy with the hair as blonde as hers. He was very well behaved and often complimented her on her appearance. "Mama, your hair looks so pretty!" he'd say, beaming up at her when she'd finished arranging her hair.

"Thank you, Ambrose. Aren't you a sweet boy?" She'd smile at him as she placed the brush on the vanity table.

Ambrose was Gretchen's little shadow, day in and day out. He was fascinated with her sewing and begged to learn how to sew himself. It briefly crossed Gretchen's mind that her older boys wanted to follow daddy – not mommy – and swing a hammer like their carpenter father, but shrugged it off and told herself each child was different. She firmly believed that each person had different talents. Perhaps Ambrose was more of an artist, so Ambrose learned to sew.

After she'd taken the children to get their photos taken, Gretchen decided that Ambrose might someday be involved in the theater or the performing arts. Stewart, Gilbert, and Augustine – the boys' baby sister, who was two years younger than Ambrose – all had their photos taken first. Gretchen knew Ambrose would not only be patient as he waited, but that he'd look perfectly groomed whether he waited two minutes or two hours. Therefore, she had his photo taken last. As he entertained himself by playing quietly with the costumes and props, Gretchen had an inkling that Ambrose's future involved show business. When his time came, Ambrose posed perfectly with a cap and cane, wearing a snowy ruffled collar. Gretchen loved that photo and cherished it all the years of her life.

Not only did Ambrose learn to sew, he became a designer at a young age as well. By the time he was six, he was sketching designs for clothing, which he'd then sew for Augustine's doll. Auggie, as the family called her, had the best-dressed doll in town, and all her playmates were green with envy over her doll, Mattie's, fashions. They complained that their stupid brothers only put spiders in their beds and tried to break their dolls; they never dressed their dolls so beautifully, like Ambrose did.

The boys at school, including his twin brothers Stewart and Gilbert, called Ambrose a sissy - partly because of his sewing and designing skills, partly because he was pale and stayed inside with his mother so much, and partly because virtually all his friends at school were girls. Ambrose preferred playing with his girl friends at recess, a fact that was not overlooked by the boys, who seemed to revel in torturing those who were different. They tried to taunt him by chanting, "Do you know Ambrose? He's as dainty as a rose!"

Ambrose simply replied, "Say what you want. Am I really supposed to care what you think of me?" Stumped, the boys would leave him alone for a while, not knowing Ambrose and his mother had crafted that response for the sole purpose of silencing their taunts.

Stewart and Gilbert never teased him again after the first time they had joined in with the others; their father had taken the belt to them when he and Gretchen had found out they'd been involved. The twins still thought Ambrose was an oddball, but they learned to keep those thoughts to themselves – at least in public.

In an effort to become a slightly smaller target, Ambrose started spending a bit more time doing "typical" boy things. Ambrose didn't get involved in rough-and-tumble activities like football or wrestling around in the dirt – he did like to stay clean – but he excelled at anything that involved aim and precision. Soon the boys who'd teased him were sorry they'd opened their mouths as Ambrose became a master at marbles, archery, and the slingshot. He could whittle a piece of wood into just about anything and was also great at strategy-based games like checkers and chess. Ambrose played checkers and chess with his father, Walter, which finally gave them a common ground to meet upon since Walter wanted nothing to do with the sewing in which Ambrose had become so immersed.

As the years passed and puberty took hold, Ambrose began to notice that he wasn't girl crazy like the other boys. He found many females aesthetically pleasing, and loved to look at their hair and clothes, but he had no interest in doing the dirty things Stewart and Gilbert whispered and joked about in the bedroom the three boys shared. He'd heard the phrase "late bloomer" and figured it applied to him. However, by the time he was sixteen and the lustful thoughts and feelings about girls hadn't taken hold, he was truly concerned. When he developed a crush on a classmate - a male classmate - Ambrose was terrified. He didn't want to be different. He was already a bit of an outcast and didn't want to be a "sissy boy." He didn't want the twins and the others to be right.

Most of all, he didn't want to go to Hell. Ambrose had attended church weekly since he could remember. Now he began to fear for his very soul. He always listened to the sermons very carefully and knew that any relationship aside from a marriage between a man and a woman wasn't recognized in the eyes of God - wasn't recognized by anyone he knew, as a matter of fact. Ambrose felt utterly alone. In whom could he confide? He was alone in facing this alarming difference. He was sure no one in his hometown of Spring Valley was afflicted the way he was. Ambrose decided he'd just ignore the feelings. He also decided to pray that he'd be saved when Judgment Day came – that somehow God would have mercy on his soul.

Ignoring his feelings worked – for a while. He squashed down his feelings for the handsome and broad-shouldered Mitchell Taggart, who was in his English class, and focused on schoolwork and design. He was particularly good at adding detailed beadwork to his creations, and his mother Gretchen planted a seed in his mind to go to New York after he graduated high school.

"Ambrose, you have such talent. You should go to New York and work in clothing design or costume design. I think you'd be marvelous in the wardrobe department of a theater!"

Ambrose was startled. "New York? But that's so far away from here, from you." He furrowed his brow, simultaneously intrigued and frightened by the idea.

"Ambrose, you know it hurts me to say such a thing, thinking of you leaving Michigan and of us being apart, but a mother has to do what's best for her children – not for herself. I think you've got a bigger life ahead of you – a different life ahead of you than this small town can offer. New York City is even bigger and better than Detroit, where we've visited your Aunt Ellen. I'm certain you could find work in New York. Plus, then I'd have an exciting place to come visit you!"

Ambrose was hard pressed to imagine living without his mother nearby, given the close bond they shared, but she assured him they'd stay in touch through frequent letters and that they'd visit each other in person at least twice a year. He trusted his mother and would follow her advice in this, just as he'd taken her advice when it came to dealing with the schoolyard bullies. He became both resigned to and excited about the prospect of his new life in New York.

As Ambrose's final year of high school drew to a close, they braced themselves for goodbye. On the day the family saw Ambrose off at the train station, Gretchen hugged her handsome blonde son for a long time and tried not to cry, but failed. He struggled to hold back tears and succeeded, but only because his father and twin brothers were watching. He also hugged Auggie and promised to keep her up to date on fashion trends in New York City. When he turned to Gretchen a final time, she pressed an envelope into his hand and whispered, "Open this on the train, my darling son." Ambrose hugged her hard once more, then strode quickly to the train. He stuck his hand out the window to wave as the train started to move, and then they were gone.

When Ambrose was comfortably settled into his seat and the train moving at a steady pace, he opened the envelope his mother had given him. The first thing he pulled out was a thin braid of her blonde hair. The ends were tied with bits of narrow ribbon. There was also a note.

Dear Ambrose,

I couldn't possibly love you any more than I do, dear son. From the time you were a young boy complimenting me on my hair to today – leaving for the city to work in the field in which you're so very skilled – you've brought me such joy. I wish you happiness, health, love, and success, Ambrose. You are truly a treasure. Every mother and father should be lucky enough to have a son like you.
Love,
Mother

Ambrose couldn't hold back the tears anymore and grasped his mother's hair tightly in his hand as he sped toward his destination – and his destiny.

It worked out just as Gretchen had hoped. Ambrose was soon employed at a major theater in New York City. He rented a room relatively near to where he worked and focused on honing his skills and gaining experience. During this time, Ambrose finally discovered others like himself – men who were attracted to other men. It seemed the theater was full of them, in fact. The first time one of the male cast members flirted openly with him, Ambrose nearly died of shock. The man was handsome and otherwise appealing, but Ambrose was mortified. Not knowing what to do, he just ignored the flirtation completely.

However, after he'd been working at the theater long enough, it was clear that he was one of many, and that it wasn't considered a very big deal to have the feelings and attractions that Ambrose felt. It was certainly still a big deal in the outside world, where being homosexual could lead to insults, beatings, or even death, but in the theater it seemed par for the course.

It was a relief to know he wasn't alone, but Ambrose was still uncomfortable with it all – with this difference within. He wished with all his heart that he could be "normal" – that he could have a wife, children, a romantic relationship that didn't have to be hidden. He wanted what all the heterosexual people had: the right to get married and the ability to express affection in public. Just to be sure that he really was gay – to leave no stone unturned - Ambrose had sex with a woman. He barely got through the ordeal and swore never to do such a thing again.

Despite his longing for "the norm," Ambrose knew he could never pretend to be something he wasn't. He knew he'd never court a woman, marry her, and have children with her if that wasn't true to his heart. To do so would be dishonest, and he couldn't imagine dragging some unsuspecting woman into a lie of such magnitude. Ambrose was willing to be alone, if need be, rather than create a fictitious life for the sake of convenience and appearances.

Over time, after the shocking same-sex flirtation he'd experienced, he had a few flings - one with a dancer named Larry who was in the chorus and one with the male lead in an operetta they'd staged – but he hadn't found love and wasn't really the promiscuous type. Ambrose sometimes wondered if he'd spend his life alone. He needn't have worried.

His mother had written to say her friend's son, Kenneth, was moving to the city from Ohio. She hoped her son would show Kenneth around the city a bit and help him to settle in.

> *I know you remember how daunting New York City can be to the uninitiated, given you're a fairly recent transplant. It would mean a lot to me, and to Kenneth's mother, Carole, if you'd lend a hand and serve as the welcoming committee.*

Ambrose responded to his mother's letter the very same day he received it.

Dear Mother,

Of course I'll meet Kenneth and show him around. We're quite busy at the theater getting ready to open our latest production, and I feel as though I'm nearly blind from beading the female lead's bodice for the finale, but I'd be glad to help. Perhaps a glimpse of life outside the costume shop will do me good. I'll meet his train Friday as requested and will give Kenneth your regards.

All my love,
Ambrose

Ambrose met the train, as promised, and held up a small sign that read "Kenneth Davies" so he wouldn't miss the one person he was trying to find. Kenneth turned out to be a very pleasant surprise in the looks department. When he stopped in front of Ambrose, Ambrose felt his heartbeat quicken as he took in the stranger's tall frame, trim but muscled physique, and handsome face. Kenneth's most compelling feature was his deep brown eyes. The crinkles around them winked at Ambrose when he smiled, which transfixed Ambrose and momentarily deafened him.

Ambrose suddenly realized that Kenneth had spoken and was waiting for an answer. "Pardon me?" Ambrose tried not to blush, and told himself that Kenneth couldn't possibly know what he was thinking and wouldn't possibly suspect his attraction.

"I said I'm Kenneth Davies. Are you Ambrose?" Kenneth smiled again, and the crinkles returned.

"Yes, I am! Sorry – I couldn't hear you there for a second. It's so loud in here." Ambrose made a quick recovery and tried to appear calm and in control. "It's so nice to meet you, Kenneth. How was your trip?"

"It wasn't too bad, if you don't count the baby that screamed its way across the entire state of Pennsylvania." He chuckled and rolled his eyes heavenward. "I'm looking forward to washing up after this long trip and to getting settled into my room. It's so kind of you to show me the way. You can call me Ken, by the way. Only my mother calls me Kenneth."

"And mine too, apparently. My mother, Gretchen, sends her regards. I'm glad to help – it's no trouble. The rooming house you've picked out isn't too far from here. You'll be refreshed and resting in no time. You're actually a few blocks from where I room, so I know the neighborhood well."

What began as courtesy from one family friend to another soon developed into a strong friendship. Ambrose kept telling himself that it could only ever be friendship, but he knew that he was falling deeper in love with Ken each time he saw him. He braced himself for the day when Ken would introduce him to some young woman he'd started dating. It would be a dagger to the heart, one that he'd have to bear somehow. Ambrose knew that unrequited love could be a frequent visitor in his life.

Ken was a wonderful friend, so in addition to longing for a romantic relationship, Ambrose didn't want to lose his company. From time to time they'd meet for lunch as they worked near each other. Ken would listen attentively to the stories Ambrose would tell. There was nearly as much drama backstage at a theater company as there was onstage, and Ken seemed to revel in it as much as Ambrose did. Ken, in turn, would tell stories about the accounting firm where he worked. Although the subject matter was definitely blander and the characters more restrained than some of the outlandish theater folk, there was plenty of office drama and politics to keep Ambrose up to date on.

Some of their best times were spent at Ambrose's place, a moderate-sized room in which he'd arranged and decorated everything just so. His clothes were impeccably arranged in his wardrobe, and framed posters from the shows he'd done costume work on lined the walls, along with a family portrait taken shortly before Ambrose had left his hometown. He had a small library in the bottom shelves of a bookshelf while he used the upper shelves as a small bar. Ambrose and Ken often put a record on the phonograph, poured a few drinks, and smoked cigarettes until the air was hazy and full. They talked for hours, about anything and everything. They often sat next to each other on Ambrose's bed, shoes off and backs leaned up against the wall.

Occasionally their arms would accidentally touch or they'd nudge each other in jest. Although such touches appeared to be an innocent act, Ambrose's body would become taut with a tingling sensation that he desperately tried to suppress. He was terrified that Ken would discover his true feelings and afraid of how his friend would react. However, Ambrose wasn't the first to tip his hand and share his true feelings.

"Ambrose, you're one hell of a friend. I'm a lucky guy to have such a good friend here in this crazy city." Both Ken and Ambrose had downed several shots on this particular night, and Ken was a bit freer with his speech and with physical affection than he usually was. "You're the best thing that's happened to me, Ambrose." He said this while looking into Ambrose's eyes.

Ambrose almost believed he meant it in a romantic way, but he knew he had to be mistaken in his interpretation. "You silly bastard, you've had a lot to drink. It's a good thing you don't have far to go to get home – you'd likely get lost and end up asleep in some alley!" Ambrose tried to joke, to dissolve any undercurrents he might be imagining, and stood to pour himself more scotch.

Ken rose too, swayed slightly on his feet, and grabbed onto Ambrose as if to steady himself. They stood facing each other, blue eyes burning into brown, until Ken leaned forward, their lips meeting as their eyes closed of their own volition. That one kiss changed their lives forever. It was the first time Ken had kissed a man and the first time Ambrose had kissed a man he loved.

Years later, when they looked back on the moment after that first kiss, Ken would tease his partner by saying Ambrose looked both flushed and pale all at the same time. Ambrose's feelings were, in fact, somewhat contradictory. He was thrilled that his affections were returned, but was also stunned that Ken – whom he'd thought was straight – could have feelings for another man. Apparently Ken had been fighting his feelings and his true nature for years, but once he and Ambrose became so close he knew he didn't want to fight any more. He was ready to love.

Ambrose too had found peace and contentment. He no longer feared God's wrath. He knew he was as God made him, and God didn't make mistakes. Although Ambrose lost his dear mother five years after his move to New York City, he liked to think she checked in on him from time to time – at least twice yearly as she'd promised. He could feel her especially close when he pulled the braid of her blonde hair from the original envelope in which she'd given it to him. He reread her last letter from time to time, the one that had arrived shortly before her unexpected passing. He was particularly fond of the last paragraph.

So many people are concerned with fitting in and fulfilling expectations put upon them by society. While you've been responsible and have followed the "standard" course of things in many ways – school, job, etc. – I suspect you've forged a slightly different path in other ways. Always know I'm proud of you, Ambrose, and am proud of the man you've become. May you always find happiness by following your heart, not the edicts of others.

He and his mother had never spoken plainly about him being homosexual, but in his heart he knew she was aware and was happy for him, despite the differences in his life that she couldn't have imagined when she gave birth to him. Ambrose knew she still wished him happiness, health, love, and success, as she had all those years ago — no matter that the love he'd found was a slightly different kind of love.

Two Angels

"Son of a gun!"

A red dot of blood appeared on Adriane Scott's finger, evidence of the minor self-inflicted wound. She quickly stuck her finger in her mouth to suck the blood off so she wouldn't stain the blanket she was embroidering. She glanced over at her son, Sean Thomas, who was sleeping nearby, and was relieved to see he hadn't been disturbed by her sudden outburst. He slept on, mercifully unaware of the small annoyances and major catastrophes that can affect one's life in a single hour. His mother wouldn't be so lucky.

Adriane drank in the sight of her precious child for a moment more before returning her attention to the project at hand and the offending embroidery needle that had just pierced her flesh. She smiled, thinking of her husband, Sam. He was so loving and kind and so patient with her somewhat challenged housekeeping skills. She'd been working on the blanket for Sean Thomas last night after dinner as well, and Sam had tried to assure her that her embroidery stitches were improving all the time.

"Sam, you're very sweet — and a terrible liar! I've been trying to embroider this yellow duck on Sean Thomas' blanket, but it doesn't look anything like a duck — no matter what you say." Adriane had frowned at her evening's work, sorely tempted to throw it into the wood-burning stove.

"Okay, okay. I'll admit the duck looks a bit odd - if you admit that the border is progressing nicely. You've really got those blue x's down well, honey!" Sam grinned; his blue eyes twinkled at her. She'd chosen the blue border thread to match Sam's eye color — his eyes made a striking combination with his brown hair. "Give yourself some more time, Adriane. Your handiwork will improve. In the meantime, Sean Thomas and I appreciate your efforts, even if they aren't always perfect."

This positive "glass-is-half-full" outlook was one of Sam's dominant character traits, and Adriane had valued it immensely as they'd progressed through the first two years of their marriage. He never became angry or impatient when she accidentally burned or undercooked a portion of their meals, and she had been improving over time. She basked in his praise and became more confident each day. The embroidery on the blanket was a perfect example; with Sam supporting her, Adriane knew she'd have it down in no time.

Today she was looking forward to Sam's arrival. He'd be home from work in a few hours. In addition to working their small farm, he worked in the nearby coal mines. He'd come home absolutely covered in black, gritty soot, with only his eyes and teeth showing white. Adriane always helped him wash up before dinner. She also took extra care washing his clothes, making sure they were always clean and well pressed – whether he was attending church or working. Each night when he crossed the threshold of their home, Adriane let out a quiet sigh of relief and silently said a prayer of thanks that her beloved had come home to her safely. Working in the mines was incredibly dangerous, what with the deadly gases, explosions, and cave-ins, and it was all Adriane could do to not beg Sam to skip work each day. She couldn't imagine life without him, and every day she prayed she'd never have to. If God heard Adriane's prayers, he chose to ignore them for purposes only he was privy to.

Adriane heard a wagon pull up out front and, with a quick glance at the still-sleeping Sean Thomas, she went to investigate. When she saw her mother outside, climbing down from the wagon with her father's help, her heart dropped. It wasn't like her folks to be away from their small mercantile in the middle of a weekday afternoon, even if one of their employees was also working the day shift. Another movement caught her eye, and she saw Matt Sloane's wagon approaching from the left. Matt was driving, but Sam was nowhere to be seen – and they always traveled to and from the mine together.

Adriane stepped outside as her mother, Rose, drew near. Adriane nervously said, "Hi Mama, what brings you by at this time of day? Couldn't stay away from your grandson?" Her voice wavered, as if sensing what was about to fall down upon her. Adriane had never seen such a bleak look on her mother's face. Adriane's father joined them, and her parents glanced at each other as if bracing themselves for a coming storm before turning back to their youngest child.

"Adriane, there was an accident at the mine." Her mother spoke slowly and deliberately, as if she was trying to make the incomprehensible somehow tolerable. "A deadly accident. Sam…" Her voice choked and caught in her throat, and the heartache she couldn't manage to voice to her daughter came pouring out of her eyes in a thick river of tears.

Adriane was stunned and disbelieving. Her mother was implying that Sam – her Sam, the love of her life – was…what, hurt? Seriously hurt? It seemed to be even worse than that, but she stared blankly at her parents, certain they were mistaken. She glanced at Matt Sloane's wagon and saw canvas covering something in its bed. When she looked at Matt's face, Adriane knew Sam was gone. Widely regarded as one of the toughest son-of-a-bitches in Carbon County, Matt was crying like a little boy, the only clean parts of his face were salt-water streaks that stretched from his red-rimmed eyes to his chin. He couldn't even look at Adriane, just stared at the reins in his hands and sobbed silently – his chest convulsing with each breath. Adriane's parents continued to stare at her, waiting for the onslaught of her anguish. They didn't have to wait long at all.

Heaving sobs burst forth from her chest, and her hands squeezed into fists convulsively at her sides. Adriane felt huge waves of pain wash over her, threatening to drown her. "Nooooo!" she half-sobbed, half-screamed. "No, no, no - not my Sam!" Adriane looked like a wild and wounded animal as her eyes shot to what she suddenly realized was Sam's covered body in the back of Matt's wagon. She dodged her parents, ran to the wagon, and clambered up into it, ignoring her parents' and Matt's shouts to stop. She pulled back the canvas sheeting to reveal the cool, still body of her husband.

Black with soot as he was, Adriane couldn't see any obvious injury; she started shaking him desperately. "Wake up, Sam, wake up! I need you – Sean Thomas needs you. Wake up sweetie, please." When her prodding and urging yielded no results, Adriane looked at her parents with eyes that screamed out her pain and her reluctance to accept the situation for what it was.

"I'm so sorry Adriane, but he's gone," her father said softly, his jaw clenching repeatedly in order to stave off the tears that threatened.

Adriane collapsed in a heap on Sam's chest, alternately sobbing, screeching, and wailing out her pain and loss. Sam's soot-covered overalls were soon drenched with her tears, and when her parents finally raised her up and lifted her down from the wagon, her once-pristine face, skirt, and blouse were covered with a soggy mixture of coal dust and tears. When they set her on her feet, she half-fainted, so her father picked her up and carried her into the house as if she were a child.

When Adriane came to a short time later, her parents were talking in soft voices about what needed to be done.

"I'll ask my sister, Claire, if she can take care of Sean Thomas until after the funeral. I don't think Adriane will be up for it," she heard her mother say. "You and Arnold will need to do the chores here at the farm until we get things sorted out. I'll get to work making some of the food we'll need, including the funeral biscuits."

Adriane had eaten the funeral biscuits whenever a family died; they were more like shortbread cookies than actual biscuits.

Her mother paused in her instructions and took a deep pained breath. "I'll also prepare Sam's body for the funeral. Please ask Matt to bring Sam inside."

"No Mama, I'll get Sam ready." Adriane's voice sounded hollow, like a distant echo, but her folks heard her nonetheless. "I'll bathe him, and I'll dress him. He'd want me to do it." Sam would be laid out in the parlor for the services, which would take place the next day.

Worried, her parents silently assessed Adriane, trying to decide if she was up to it. Her eyes already appeared sunken, and Adriane seemed to have aged fifteen years in the fifteen minutes since she'd found out about Sam. Adriane climbed off the bed as if to show them she was capable. When her father nodded to her mother and headed for the door, Adriane knew she'd have her way.

The family pulled together, as directed by Rose, and Sean Thomas was soon sequestered at Adriane's aunt's house. Adriane must've kissed her son goodbye, but was so far removed from her normal mental state that she didn't remember doing it and didn't notice he was gone. Arnold and her father were out tending the livestock, and her mother was in the kitchen baking for the funeral when Adriane started preparing Sam's body.

How did a wife bear such loss and misery without breaking into a million brittle and jagged pieces? Adriane silently wondered to herself. Although she tried to perform her task without wailing in agony, she knew she couldn't get through it without any tears at all and settled for a steady flow of tears, copious sniffing, and the soaking of several handkerchiefs.

The sight of Sam, cold and motionless, might be the death of her, too, she thought. She wanted to be where Sam was, wherever that was. He was definitely not here in the shell of a body before her. Still, she forced herself on, washing his skin, taking care to remove every bit of coal dust from his body — as if removing any reside of the cause of his death might turn back time. Sadly it did not, and Adriane was faced with the bruises and contusions that riddled his clean skin. The explosion at the mine — the force of the blast — had killed her husband, and she shuddered to think of the gaping maw of the mine's opening that had carelessly turned out her husband's lifeless body.

When Adriane had bathed every inch of Sam's long body — he was over six feet tall — her mother came in and helped her dress him. They put him in his best suit, which he wore to church every Sunday and on other special occasions. He'd recently worn the suit when a traveling photographer had come by, and the young family had had their portrait taken in the side yard. When Adriane had seen the resulting photo, she'd teased Sam mercilessly.

"You're a fine man, Sam Scott, but you can't keep a bow tie on straight, no matter how often I straighten it for you!"

"Well, Shorty, perhaps the problem is that you're barely tall enough to reach my bow tie, let alone straighten it properly!" Sam had said, chuckling. He called her Shorty from time to time, and folks in town often commented on the disparity in their heights.

"Good things come in small packages, Mr. Scott, and that's all you need to know!" Adriane had retorted playfully, winking at him.

As Adriane tied Sam's bow tie one last time, an ocean of her tears rained down upon it, spattering the fabric with spots. She was glad to know a little bit of her - a little of the essence of her sorrow - would go with Sam into the grave, soaked into the fabric of his burial clothes.

When they'd dressed him in the suit and bow tie, Adriane asked for time alone with Sam to finish up. Her mama squeezed her hand, kissed her cheek and, after assuring Adriane she'd just be in the other room, took her leave.

It was then that Adriane worked on the fine details. She lovingly put on her husband's socks and shoes, tying the latter with a neat and tight bow. She put a clean handkerchief in his pocket, double-checked his bow tie, and then moved on to his hair. Before combing it, she cut off a small lock from a spot that wouldn't show at the viewing, tied the hair with some of the blue embroidery thread that matched Sam's eyes, and tucked the hair into her jewelry box. Finally, she liberally applied some of his favorite aftershave, then tucked that away too.

The tears continued raining down her face as they'd been doing since Adriane had started this agonizing and tender task. Looking down at him, so handsome even in death, she nearly hyperventilated, still unable to accept the fact that the earth would swallow him up the following day and she'd never see him again. She bent to gently kiss his lips, remembering the love and passion they'd shared, but the chill and unresponsiveness she found there cut her to the bone. Unable to hold herself upright any longer, Adriane kneeled beside the bed where Sam lay and wept into the clothing she'd so carefully arranged.

Rose came in a short while later and found her daughter sobbing over her husband's body. Rose would've willingly given her own life to take away Adriane's pain. Instead, she gently took Adriane by the shoulders, guided her to the couch in the living room, and tucked a blanket around her. Rose eased her slight body down next to Adriane, afraid that jostling her would somehow cause even more damage to her daughter's wounded heart, and gently drew her daughter into her arms.

Rose had a lovely voice and had always sung to her children when they were young. When Adriane had been frightened by nightmares, Rose would fold her into her arms and hum a wordless tune, gently stroking her hair at the same time. It had worked every time, relaxing Adriane enough that she'd fall asleep again, untroubled. Although Rose knew she wouldn't be able to fix anything for her cherished daughter, she held her, sang to her, and stroked her hair anyway. Adriane quieted, and her body slowly relaxed in her mother's arms. She didn't fall asleep, but the storm of tears quieted and stilled.

Knowing that this hollowed-out version of her daughter needed sustenance, although Adriane likely had no interest in eating, Rose bustled off to the kitchen, returning with a tray. She handed Adriane some tea that she'd spiked with a splash of whiskey, then sat next to Adriane as she sipped vacantly. Next Rose had her eat a butter and jam sandwich she'd made so her daughter would have something to fuel her physically and emotionally taxed little body. She was glad Adriane had managed to stop crying, but her empty stare worried Rose more than the tears had.

Adriane leaned back against the sofa and silently stared at the blanket she'd been happily embroidering mere hours ago. She'd been a whole person then and marveled at how quickly life's gifts could be taken away without warning.

The funeral was a veritable fog for Adriane. She wasn't sure who brought the flowers that filled their home, who had prepared all the food the mourners would partake of, or even how she'd gotten dressed or arranged her hair. She assumed that her mother had seen to all of the details, likely calling on lady friends to bring in flowers from their gardens. Friends, family, and others they knew had undoubtedly stopped by with food prior to the service, ensuring plenty of refreshments for those in attendance.

Adriane found herself in the parlor, sitting in the chair nearest to Sam, who had been laid out for viewing and for the services. Numb – that's what she was. She was numb, except that she was also filled with so much anxiety and sorrow that her heart tried to leap out of her chest. In a distant part of her mind she recognized that people had started to arrive and that she'd probably responded to those offering their condolences, but the details didn't register. Nothing but the reality of Sam's death was sinking in.

Rose had done her best to ensure that the funeral was a lovely, if sad affair. She had seen to every detail, from thanking the preacher for the services to guiding guests to the refreshments and making sure they received one of the funeral biscuits she'd made the night before. A family tradition dating back to Colonial times, Rose had used the heirloom shortbread-like recipe to make a round cookie for each guest. She'd used her ceramic cookie press to stamp a heart into each one, keeping the family tradition alive and trying to bring the tiniest bit of sweetness to such a sorrowful day. Rose wouldn't allow herself the luxury to grieve herself until she'd taken care of everything for her daughter.

The burial itself was just as awful as the young, grieving widow had expected it to be. As they lowered Sam's rough wooden coffin into the grave, Adriane didn't know if she would ever look at soil again without pain. The sight of newly turned soil might remain a thorn in her heart for the rest of her days. She couldn't even think of one tomorrow without Sam, let alone hundreds or thousands – her heart was surely intertwined with his down in the silent darkness.

Two days after the funeral, Adriane was still in a grief-induced stupor. She was trying desperately not to think or feel. When the thoughts did creep in, they were grim. Adriane envisioned herself clawing through the blackness to curl up next to Sam, never to move again.

Sean Thomas was home again, back from Aunt Claire's, and Rose was forced to care for both her daughter and her grandson because of Adriane's lethargy and depression. Rose kept hoping the old Adriane would return, perhaps after her daughter awoke from one of her many naps. It seemed all Adriane did was sleep, or sit silently and stare off into the distance with tears streaming down her cheeks.

Rose put both Adriane and Sean Thomas down for a nap – Adriane on the sofa, and Sean Thomas in his playpen. "Adriane, I have to go out briefly, but I'll be back from my errand soon – hopefully before you and Sean Thomas wake up." Her daughter nodded slightly at her words, but her eyes were already closed – shut against the world again. Rose planted a soft kiss on Adriane's forehead and went out.

Adriane hadn't really grasped her mother's words; they'd almost sounded like the buzzing of a bee flying around her head. She was already slipping into a dream. Sam was there, for the first time since he'd died. Her dream was more of a memory, actually – a trip back to the previous year when she'd still been pregnant, about eight months along. It was a warm summer's night early in the season. Sam had drawn her down to the river that ran parallel to their property, guiding her carefully lest she trip, although the moonlight was shining brightly. They reached a spot at the river where the bank sloped gently and shed their clothes before wading in. The water was cool, but not frigid, and it refreshed their skin as they relaxed against the gentle caress of the current.

They'd talked together softly, of their hopes and dreams, and spoke of their unborn child. Sam picked her up in his arms like she was a bride being carried over a threshold, and Adriane's swollen belly glimmered in the moonlight, water streaming down the sides as she surfaced. The baby had moved and kicked then, making its presence known in the quiet that was only broken by the murmur of their beating hearts and the crickets calling to each other in the night. They'd smiled at each other delightedly upon seeing the undulation of her belly and the proof of life within, and they sealed the magic of the moment with an electric kiss that left them both dizzy.

Adriane sat upright, shocked from her sleep as if she'd been struck by lightning. The sweet memory of the dream filled her mind and her heart with utter despair as reality drove home the cruel reminder: Her true love was lost forever.

Without hesitation, Adriane rose and moved to the wardrobe in her bedroom. She pulled on Sam's heavy wool coat, which pooled on the floor because she was so petite. Her plan of action was clear in her mind. She'd walk to the river, loading the large coat pockets with rocks as she went. She'd go to the deepest part of the river, near to where she and Sam had bathed in the moonlight, and walk in. Adriane had never learned to swim and prayed her body would give out quickly when it was completely submerged in the water. She wasn't thinking of it as suicide, simply a way to rejoin her husband – immediately.

As she turned and headed toward the front door, Adriane was hit with a flood of sound so earsplitting that it snatched her from her from the dark recesses into which she'd fallen. Turning her head to the left, she saw Sean Thomas standing at the rails of his playpen, screaming with such violence that Adriane thought he must be on fire or a victim of some other sort of torture. Her mild-mannered child never screamed like that, and it made Adriane's heart beat faster to hear him so upset. She rushed over and picked him up immediately, giving him a once-over and searching for the source of his discontent.

Seeing nothing obviously awry, she hugged him to her, trying to comfort both her son and herself, breaking free from the wretched logjam of despair. She saw with sudden clarity that she'd nearly left her son without either a mother or a father. Sean Thomas quieted almost immediately and burrowed into his mother's arms as she rocked him.

"Shhh, it's okay, my love. Mama's here." Adriane held him even more tightly. "It's okay, Sean Thomas, it's going to be okay. Mama won't leave you." She still couldn't imagine how she'd face a future without Sam, but Adriane knew she was telling her son the truth. She would never leave him of her own volition. She'd fight tooth and nail to stay with her precious son to see him grow up to be a man.

When Rose entered the home, her heart lifted to see Sean Thomas in her daughter's arms. It seemed as though Adriane was present in her body again and that she also had presence of mind.

Later, after Sean Thomas was in bed for the night, Adriane cried penitent tears as she told her mother what she'd nearly done. "How could I have taken even one step toward that river? My poor baby! Sam would've been so disappointed."

Adriane wasn't flushing out her sentences, but her mother understood her heart. Adriane was consumed with guilt and shame, having nearly left her innocent child an orphan, and Rose had to pry Adriane's hands loose from where they covered her face.

"Adriane, you have to forgive yourself. You were wrecked with grief – so torn up over the loss of Sam that you weren't in your right mind for a spell. You are a good mother, and everyone who knows you knows you'd lay down your life to protect that child. Sometimes life throws things at us that we can hardly bear, and losing Sam is that way for you. As sure as I know you're going to continue to shed tears in mourning, I also know you're going to continue to heal.

You're going to be a bit stronger every day, and part of the joy you're going to find in life is your son. You'll help him through, and he'll help you through."

Adriane smiled her love and thanks to her mother, knowing she was truly blessed to have her.

That night Adriane dreamed of Sam again, but this dream was quite different. It seemed more like a visit. She saw his handsome face and twinkling blue eyes and drank in the sight of him while taking in the words he said as well.

"Sorry to leave you so soon, Shorty, but it couldn't be helped. You know I'd never choose to leave. You're going to have to be brave for me and for Sean Thomas, okay? I promise we'll all be together again, one day...." He faded from her sight as the last word faded into silence, and Adriane slept on peacefully.

Adriane and her mother planned to do the wash the next day, part of an effort to ease Adriane back into her usual routine. As she gathered Sam's dirty clothes into a laundry basket, Adriane decided she'd wash them and then pack them away for Sean Thomas, thinking he might like to have them someday. She lifted a last pair of pants, and something clattered to the floor. Adriane bent to pick it up, but paused mid-movement when she saw it was Sam's pocketknife. Bending fully to pick it up, she smiled wistfully when she held the knife on her open palm. It had belonged to Sam's father, who'd passed it down to Sam; it was a cherished, if functional, keepsake.

Adriane knew she'd pass the pocketknife on from one angel to the next. Sam was her angel in heaven, and Sean Thomas was her angel here on earth. Folks tended to think that children needed their parents so very much, but Adriane now knew with utter certainty that sometimes parents need their children just as much. She knew Sean Thomas would keep her trying when times were dark, would guide her toward the light with his innocence and joy.

Adriane abandoned the laundry basket where it was and tucked the pocketknife into her jewelry box with Sam's lock of hair. She walked into Sean Thomas' room, where he was playing quietly with his wooden blocks. Adriane scooped him up and went to sit in the rocker by his crib. She began to tell him about his daddy, about their love for each other, and about their love for him, their cherished son. Adriane vowed she'd always tell her son stories about his father — what a happy lot there was to share.

ACKNOWLEDGEMENTS

I'd like to begin by thanking my husband, José Nuñez. My best friend and creative partner in crime, he always challenges me to grow and improve. Thank you, dear hubby, for all your love and support. I also appreciate you bringing your talent and skill to this project, by designing the book's cover, handling the book's layout, taking the photos of my illustrations, and by taking my headshot. Team Nuñez!

I offer my deepest thanks and much love to my family and friends, and to all those who have encouraged me, challenged me, and helped me along the way in my life.

I'd also like to thank those who read the earliest versions of these stories: Terry Parker, Beth Nielsen and Carie Quigley. Thanks to my editor, Nanette Day, for helping me to tidy and polish. Thanks to Phil Weigand-DiNicola for his insight, which helped ensure the authenticity of one of the stories. I'd also like to thank Louise Muenstermann for the canary feathers she provided for "The Late Bloomer of Bishop" illustration.

Finally, I'd like to offer my thanks to the Public Library system. I've spent countless hours in libraries over the years, dating back to elementary school, and my love for books, reading and fiction has never waned. I wouldn't be the same person I am today without the gift of literacy and the free access I've had to books, and I'm very thankful.

The illustrations in this book were created in color, though they're shown here in black and white. To see them in all their glory, please visit my BOOK page at www.melodynunez.com. Thank you!

www.ingramcontent.com/pod-product-compliance
Lightning Source LLC
Chambersburg PA
CBHW050846180626
46814CB00007B/2647